ESCAPE FROM KOSZALIN

ESCAPE FROM KOSZALIN

BY

ULF JENSEN

iUniverse, Inc.
New York   Bloomington

iUniverse books may be ordered through booksellers or by contacting:

iUniverse
1663 Liberty Drive
Bloomington, IN 47403
www.iuniverse.com
1-800-Authors (1-800-288-4677)

Because of the dynamic nature of the Internet, any Web addresses or links contained in this book may have changed since publication and may no longer be valid. The views expressed in this work are solely those of the author and do not necessarily reflect the views of the publisher, and the publisher hereby disclaims any responsibility for them.

ISBN: 978-1-4401-4459-2 (sc)
ISBN: 978-1-4401-4461-5 (ebook)
ISBN: 978-1-4401-4460-8 (hc)

Printed in the United States of America

iUniverse rev. date: 8/7/2009

This book is dedicated to the memory of my father
Pastor Kai Kirkegaard-Jensen,
one of the leaders of the
Danish Resistance on the island of Bornholm
and responsible for the success of the
Escape of Jews from Poland.
This is the untold story of dedication and heroism
by the Danish and Polish freedom fighters and
fishermen that saved thousands of Jewish lives
during the last two years of World War II.
During that time, Pastor Kirkegaard-Jensen
was on the Nazis' "black list"
to be shot on sight.
He constantly eluded the Nazis and was later
knighted by the King of Denmark
for his services to his country.

CHAPTER 1

The sea was pitch black.

They were ten miles off shore, and no light was seen.

High clouds obscured a nail-edged moon, and an eerie silence had displaced the rippling sound of the waves.

Captain Jay was chatting softly with his crew, when small waves began lapping against his fishing boat.

Something was approaching.

Was it a new weather front or perhaps another boat?

Suddenly the silence was shattered by a harsh German command that shot across the quiet sea.

"Halt! Abtrennen! Gleich!" (Stop! Shut down now!)

In spite of the quiet night, no one had noticed the stealth approach of the German patrol boat.

"Now where did they come from?" asked a crewman.

"Out of nowhere! They're always patrolling this coast for traders in contraband." Jay answered.

"Like what?"

"Mainly weapons for resistance fighters."

"You mean us?"

"You got that right."

"But that's not fair. We're just out here trying to make a living. We're always being stopped and searched.

"We're easy targets just drifting around looking for fish."

"It scares me every time."

"Why? They never find anything." Jay assured.

"Yeah, but you never know what kind of mood those Nazis are in."

"So?"

"All you need is for them to be in a bad mood, and a simple search could easily escalate into a deadly confrontation."

"I know. These boardings are always high-risk affairs."

"That's why I'm scared. I mean someone could easily get shot and killed at the whim of an officer."

"You worry too much"

"That's easy for you to say. You're an old hand at this sort of thing."

"Shh, here they come. We're in for a search again," Jay whispered, then shouted quickly, "We're shut down! We're just drifting!"

"Hände hoch jemand! Oder wir schiessen!"

Another harsh and unnecessary command shot across the black sea, as all aboard the small fishing boat stood up quickly, raising their hands.

Jay protested, "Don't shoot! We don't have any weapons. We don't shoot the fish; we only catch them with a net. Can we put our hands down now?"

"Very well," the officer agreed.

By now the German patrol boat had turned on all lights and come alongside the small Polish fishing boat. A Nazi officer, two German soldiers and two police dogs all crowded onto the small deck of the fishing boat.

Jay tried to maintain control of the "surprise" boarding.

"Just what're you looking for, or should I say what're they looking for?" Jay asked pointing to the two dogs that had immediately started to sniff around.

"We're looking for anything that doesn't belong on a fishing boat. The dogs are extremely good at finding such things!" Came the arrogant reply.

"Well, we don't have anything aboard that doesn't belong here."

"Good! Then you won't mind if we look around, do you?"

"No, go right ahead."

Just then the boat lurched from a passing wave. A crewmember seized the opportunity to inconspicuously drop a couple of red rags from the engine room onto the deck near the dogs. Unaware that the rags had a secret chemical that would paralyze their noses, the dogs instantly lunged at them with great interest and sniffed them violently.

"No, get back!" One of the soldiers commanded the dogs as they strained at their leashes.

"I'm sorry, said the crewmember, I lost my footing and had to let go of the rags to hold on."

"No matter," the soldier snapped, as he let the dogs continue sniffing around.

"What's in there?" the officer asked, pointing to a large square locker in front of the pilot house.

"That's where we store the fish," Jay explained as he opened the side of the locker, revealing a large tray half full of fish.

"That's not very many fish!" the officer noted.

"I know. It's not been a good night. As you can see, we have a lot of empty trays stacked in there, waiting for a better night!"

"What's behind those trays?"

"More trays, all stacked together like this," Jay pulled out a few trays in a carefree manner, showing there was nothing behind them.

"Pull out some more trays," demanded the officer who was becoming more eager.

Did he think he was onto something? Jay thought.

Jay pulled out two more trays, and the locker space appeared deeper still with more trays seen in the back.

"What about those trays?"

"What about them?"

"What's behind them?"

"More trays! We could go all the way to the back, but we rarely have to use all of the trays stacked in there."

"Pull out one more," the officer insisted, as he pulled out his automatic pistol and pointed it directly at Jay.

"Why do you guys always pull out a pistol?" Jay asked.

"We always need to be prepared."

"Prepared for what?"

"A sudden attack of resistance," came the terse reply.

"What, from us? Come on now officer, you don't really believe that, do you?"

"You never know. Some people react like a cornered animal, becoming desperate and exceedingly violent in a last ditch effort to survive. We're always ready for that."

Jay shook his head in simulated disbelief.

"OK, one more." Jay strained and crouched as he went to the back of the locker and reached for the last tray.

As he scrambled back out, the Nazis, dogs and all, poked their heads into the locker to get a good look at what he might be hiding.

This was the moment of no return, a moment that could be 30 seconds away from sudden death.

In fact, sudden death was just one inch away, the mere thickness of a wooden board!

One last board.

The board of death!

Jay blinked his eyes and stared down at the deck in an effort to calm his crew. They were close to exploding from fear that the secret hiding place was about to be revealed, and it took all the concentration they could muster to remain casual and not let their body language betray their fear. They rolled their eyes and cast fleeting glimpses at each other and Jay, and then stared at the Nazis, who pushed themselves backwards out of the locker, disappointed and bored that there was nothing there.

"Satisfied now?" Jay asked.

Without saying a word, the officer turned around and walked over to the railing. He stood there for a few moments as if in a trance, not quite sure he believed what had just happened. His face, visibly contorted from inner conflict, gave no clue about his next action, only that it might be violent.

He suddenly whirled around.

Jay and his crew held their breath.

"Very well, then! If there was anything here, the dogs would've found it. Go ahead and fish."

Turning to the soldiers he commanded, "Zurück!"

The boarding party left without further ado, disappointed in not having found anything.

The lights of the patrol boat soon vanished into the darkness of the night. Jay and his crew breathed a sigh of relief.

"Let's go," he commanded softly.

He started the engine but left the navigation lights off. He turned the wheel and pointed the bow toward their destination:

Bornholm!

A medium sized rocky Danish island, stuck far out in the Baltic Sea between Sweden and Poland, Bornholm was somewhat closer to Sweden.

"I know you guys want to race over to Bornholm," Jay resumed his chat, "but you know, we've got to be careful now. Even though we've just been boarded, it would not do to reveal our true intentions. That could be fatal for all of us."

Indeed. For Captain Jay and his two member crew and all five Jewish refugees!

Captain Jay had eluded the Nazi patrol by his wise planning and cool head during the boarding. The same could be said for his crew of two trusted friends.

They were all seasoned freedom fighters and members of the Polish Resistance.

The boat slid softly away in a whisper through the dark waters of the Baltic, very friendly this night, with a gentle breeze and small half-foot waves. Soon they were miles away from the German patrol boat, and Jay pushed the throttle all the way forward to full power. The little forty foot fisherman flew across the waves like a patrol boat.

Three hours later, Captain Jay entered a small bay with his precious cargo.

He stared intently in the direction of the beach.

The still of the night was awesome.

A few minutes went by, seemed like hours.

There was no signal anywhere.

Or was there?

Something caught his eye.

There it was again.

It was straight ahead.

A green flashing light.

It was Morse Code.

It spelled S.O.S.

A red color meant danger, but a green color was the OK signal from the Danish Resistance.

They were now in Denmark!

Chapter 2

It was a small piece of paper.
A small scrap of brown paper.
It had gone unnoticed .
Perhaps for a long time.
It passed by many eyes.
But no one saw it.
Why was it there?
Who put it there?
Why was it still there?
Many questions.
No answers.
But none were needed
The paper spoke for itself.
It had a voice.
A voice of desperation.
Time was running out.
Fast!
One boy noticed the paper.
It moved slowly past him.
Then it stopped.

He saw what none had seen.
He looked around.
No one was there.
He darted toward the train.
He was there in a flash.
It was the last car.
It was at the end of the car.
He snatched the paper off the side.
He darted back.
He hid behind a barrel.
He looked at the paper.
There was writing on it.
The words jumped off the paper.
They took his breath away.
He put it in his pocket.
He ran home,
flew up the stairs.
"Papa, Papa, look at this!"
"Where did you get this?"
"It was on the train just now!"
"Call your Mama!"
"What does it mean?"
"I'll tell you in a minute."
They all sat down.
"Joseph found this paper."
"It was on the train."
Again the words jumped off the paper.

HELP – THEY KILL US WITH GAS
THIS IS DEATH CAMP
ALL WHO COME ARE KILLED
SEPTEMBER 1943

They all gasped

"Was this on the train from Auschwitz?" The mother asked.

"Yes, it was on the side of the last car, near the end." Joseph answered.

"How can that be?" Asked the father. "How was it stuck to the train?"

"It was folded, one part was stuck with tacks, and the fold was stuck with gum."

"How did you see it?"

"I don't know. I was sitting inside the gate watching the train come in, and when it stopped, the end of the last car was right in front of me. The little paper was right there; it looked funny. I thought there might be something in it, like a little bag, you know. I didn't think anyone would mind that I grabbed it; part of it is still attached, the part with the tacks I mean."

"He's a smart boy, isn't he Rebecca?"

"Yes, perhaps a bit reckless, but it was a good thing to do. You're sure no one saw you?"

"Yes, I made sure of that. They were all up at the front of the train, except one guard closing the gate behind the train, and he didn't look my way at all."

"Good, and no one followed you home?"

"No, no, I ran as fast as I could. No one saw me; I'm sure."

"This is terrible!" said the father. Do you know what this means?"

"Tell us."

"It's the only train in and out of the Ghetto, and it's always full of people going to Auschwitz, several hundred miles south of here; but it's always empty when it returns. What this means is that we're all being lied to. We're being told that we must be relocated to a common housing area, where we can live in peace. Instead, we're sent to the gas chambers and killed. It's outrageous!"

"My God, it can't be true!?" Rebecca wailed, "maybe it's a bad joke or a prank! Maybe it's just a prank. What do you think Papa?"

"I don't think so. The letter talked to me, like God himself had spoken. The words took my breath away. I felt something go through my body. It was strange; it was truly like God touched me just then. This is no joke, Rebecca!"

"Oh, God help us!"

"What do we do, Papa"

"What can we do?" Rebecca was slipping into despair.

"We must do something. We cannot just do nothing. Let me think for a minute."

"It looks impossible," Rebecca cried, as tears streamed down her face. "I don't have much hope."

"There, there now," Papa tried to console her. "We have a great start. We've found out the truth. Without the truth we'd never have a chance. Now at least we can build on that, The truth is the corner stone of any plan for our future. Just remember that. You'll see; we'll go on from here."

"But how can we do anything?" Rebecca continued, "we're confined to this Ghetto with walls, fences and guards everywhere. We can't go out, except a few of us that have special permits. We're allowed so little contact with the outside, that help will be impossible to find. I know you're a good medical doctor, but what can you do with all this? Who can really help us? Who'll help those already in the camp?"

"Rebecca!" Joseph, Sr. looked into her eyes sternly as he grabbed her by the arms, "At least we're not yet in that camp! That gives us an edge. That gives us a chance, don't you see? Indeed, we're the only ones that still have a chance. And so the responsibility lies with us, you see! We're the ones that must find a way. We're the ones that have been chosen to find a way. We must do so!"

"What're you going to do?"

"I'm going to call a few good people together and have a meeting of the minds. I'll figure out a plan and assign the practical steps to those that can best carry them out."

"And who'll that be?"

"There's Mark, the plumber; he's also a locksmith. Then there's Aron, the banker, and…and Kaminski, yeah, Kaminski, the business man. We'll need their connections. We'll also need Wolinski, the lawyer; he's smart and trustworthy. That's it. We don't want more than that, or it'll raise suspicion."

"Do it now please, right away; don't waste a moment!"

"I'll call them right now."

CHAPTER 3

The little group of five had braved the evening curfew and gathered in Dr. Levi's second floor walk-up apartment in the center of Koszalin.

"I've asked you to come, because something very critical to our survival has just happened," Dr. Levi began.

"What's that?" They all asked.

"I got this note," he continued, "My son plucked it off the side of the last car of the train returning from Auschwitz today. Here, I'll pass it around, and you can make your own judgments. Then I'll tell you mine."

All sat in silence as they read the note and passed it around. As the note was handed back to Dr. Levi, they all broke their silence.

"It's monstrous!"

"It's inhuman!"

"It's a catastrophe!"

"As you know," Levi continued, "for thousands of years our people have struggled for survival and to return to our homeland. We and our families, along with hundreds of others of Jewish descent, have been rounded up and placed in special sections of towns, called "Ghettos", wherein we're confined until we can be taken to a so-called permanent Jewish settlement.

You may also know that during the early half of this century, many of us gravitated to Poland, and were readily accepted by the friendly Poles. We were able to assimilate into the Polish society and soon became well respected members of the country by contributing our skills and intellectual abilities. For that reason, Poland soon had the largest Jewish population of any European country."

"We know all that, so what else is new about this?"

"I've made a few calls just now and found out a lot of things. I've been so busy attending to people here that I've lost track of what's been happening outside the Ghetto. Everything's happening so fast."

"OK, so what've you found out?"

"You're keeping us in suspense!"

"During the early years of the war, our people were regularly harassed by the Nazis; and many were taken without warning to concentration camps, where they just languished, until they died of starvation.

Hitler is said to have been impatient with the progress of eliminating the Jews in his quest for "purifying" his "Aryan race" of German people. He would ask why there were still so many Jews around."

"Yes, I've heard such rumors; they were so atrocious I couldn't believe them!"

"Nor I, but listen to this," Joseph continued.

"In early 1943, it was decided by Hitler and the Nazi High Command that efforts to eliminate the Jews were to be intensified. In other words, they weren't dying fast enough, and the concentration camps were too full.

Rather than build more camps, it would be more expedient to

simply murder the Jews in the camps en- masse. It didn't take long to build halls for gassing and ovens to cremate the bodies."

"No! Is that really true?"

"Yes, and unbeknownst to all the Jewish people, including us, all Jews are to be exterminated like insects soon after arrival, all according to the capacity of the facility. They're prodded into a large hall, compelled to strip in order to shower and be "cleansed". After such thorough cleansing, poison gas is piped into the hall, and everyone is murdered. The bodies are then taken to a giant crematorium, consisting essentially of a huge oven, the vent of which is a sixty foot high smokestack. Several times a week, the crematorium is active, as seen by the smoke rising from the smokestack. As we speak, the extermination of Jews by gassing in the concentration camps is in full swing, and thousands are dying in a relatively short period of time. Actually, over one million Jews have already perished so far!"

"No! Can you believe that?"

"It's hard, but here's the worst of it, so hold onto your seats. Probably the most infamous of all the camps is the one right here in Poland, "Auschwitz"."

"Then it's true what you heard!" Mark said.

"Where did you hear all this?" Kaminski asked.

"Are you sure these are not just rumors?" Wolinski asked.

"I called a few colleagues in the Warsaw Ghetto. They heard a few things from contacts that dared speak up. They said that as time went by, Auschwitz has become known for its many atrocities. It's important for the Nazis to keep these events secret, as knowledge of them might cause our people to revolt. Therefore all communication is strictly controlled, and violators are shot on sight. There're no "human rights". There're no trials, no hearings, no consideration. There's only one right.

The Nazis have that right.

The Jews have none.

It's very simple and practical.

Violators are killed on the spot.

Then I got the note.

It spells "death" for all of us. Death for all our people."

"Are you sure the note is for real?" Asked the banker.

"It could be a prank!" Said the business man.

"Do you have any proof?" Asked the lawyer.

"I'll tell you what I think and what proof I have," said Joseph. "For someone to play a prank and jeopardize their life and risk getting caught writing and putting this note on the side of the train is unthinkable. It must have taken a lot of careful thought and planning to get this done at just the right moment and remain undiscovered. This could only have been done in all seriousness. I believe it must be for real."

"Furthermore," Joseph continued "When I first read the note, not only did the words leap off the paper and strike me right between the eyes; I felt something pierce my entire body. It was like a lightning rod. I felt instantly sick. I felt instantly afraid. I was mortified. Not just for myself, because I might soon be there myself, but for all the people already there. Death was looking me straight in the eye and smiling, as though to say, "I'll see you soon."

I felt that God himself had spoken to me. These words, as they leaped from the paper, had the power of God behind them. Not only was I convinced that they were true, but I was also convinced that they were given to me for a reason. It is as though God has chosen me to free our people. He has placed the responsibility on my shoulders. I cannot refuse. I must take up the task."

"You're right Joseph, those words are indeed a call for help from our people. We cannot ignore them."

"Yeah, yeah!"

"You all know our history. I can't pretend to be as holy as

Moses, but neither can I fail to see the parallel to the time when our people were enslaved by the Egyptians and struggled for many years to survive, only to be losing, slowly dying in captivity.

Just like Moses at that time accepted the call from God to free his people, so I feel that I've been chosen to free our people once more.

I can't refuse, and I need your help.

God guided Moses to the Promised Land, but I don't

yet see a promised land for our people.

But first things first; we must free our people.

What are your thoughts?

Do you agree with me? If so, we have no time to lose."

"We have no choice but to agree," said the business man. "This is truly a catastrophe in the making."

"Yes, I agree," the lawyer chimed in, "we've seen the problem, so now we have to fix it."

"Then we're agreed," said Joseph. "It's now up to us to free our people. We don't have a moment to lose.

"I just have to admire you, Joseph; you're always such a clear thinker. You analyze a problem, and then you take immediate action. But will we be able to save everybody?"

"I'm afraid it's impossible for us to save the people once they have been put on the train, and that'll continue to be done until the war ends. What we must try to do is help people escape from our Ghetto, so they'll not be put on this or any other train. Unfortunately, that'll only be a handful at a time. We can't have a mass exodus immediately and remain undiscovered. We must formulate a secure and practical plan."

"Mark, you're a plumber and a locksmith. You'll figure a way to let a small group of people, five or six at a time, get out of the Ghetto every night."

"Every night? That's a tall order!" Mark interrupted.

"I know, my friend, but anything less will never amount to much. Take 6 people every night for the next six months or 180 days, that's still only 1080. If we at least start with six at a time, we could perhaps find ways to double or triple that number if we're successful."

"Where'll they go after they get out?" asked the banker.

"We must get them out of Poland immediately!" Joseph continued with a serious look in his eyes.

"It's simply not possible to hide such a large number of people right under the noses of the Nazis. They must be sent out of Poland."

"But where to?" Asked the lawyer.

"It's very simple," Joseph answered. "They can't go east to Russia. They can't go west to Germany. They can't go south, hundreds of miles to Czechoslovakia and Austria, passing right by Auschwitz on the way. So what's left? They must go north!"

"North?" the group shouted in unison. "You want them to go into the ocean?"

"Their only hope is to get to a free country across the sea," Joseph continued with unabated logic. "There's only one, and that's Sweden."

"And how'll they do that?" Asked the business man.

"You can't just send them there," the lawyer argued.

Joseph turned to the business man, "Kaminski, you'll make contact with some of your connections on the outside and have them get in touch with the Swedish government as well as members of the Danish Resistance. We're going to need many resources, but principally we need a way to cross the Baltic Sea to Sweden, likely with a stopover on the Danish island of Bornholm."

"Why, you've got this all planned out already, haven't you?"

"Yes I have," Joseph continued. "Time is of essence. We'll need help from the Polish Resistance to guide the people from Koszalin to a sleepy little village like Dorlowo, just up the coast, and hide them until a fishing boat can transport them to Bornholm. We'll need a fishing boat that can transport six people every night. Once on Bornholm, the Danish Resistance must take over and hide and guide them across that island and get them on a fishing boat to Sweden."

"Do you realize what you are saying?" Wolinski asked.

"I'm open to suggestions!" Joseph retorted.

"Why not skip Bornholm and go directly to Sweden?"

"Too dangerous!" The waters are swarming with Nazi patrol boats. The fishermen can't be placed in unnecessary danger. They can't venture out of their usual fishing grounds without arousing suspicion and risk being arrested. Furthermore, the journey across the Baltic can be treacherous, and Sweden is too far away for a direct trip. Two smaller trips will be much safer and better."

"What's holding us up?" the lawyer asked.

"The main hold up will be getting the Swedes to approve. They'll need to let the people into their country at the end of the journey, and then let them mingle with the population"

"Let's get started," they all said as they got up and started to leave.

"You all know what to do.

Let's meet back here in two days and arrange a starting date."

"You sure are optimistic, Joseph," said the banker.

"No, just determined. We must act quickly."

CHAPTER 4

Promptly two days later, the little group met again in Dr. Levi's apartment. They arrived one at a time at three minute intervals and sat down in silence, waiting for the next member to arrive. On the street, not a speck of light was seen anywhere, as the Ghetto's seven-thirty curfew was in effect. Inside the apartment, the faint light from a small candle was shielded by a brown paper bag shade. No one said a word until Kaminski, the business man, arrived and sat down next to Dr. Levi, and immediately opened the discussion.

"I realize that no step in this escape plan is more important than any other," he began. "If any step fails, the whole plan may fail. However, it's apparent that the middle of the three steps, that of crossing the island of Bornholm, poses the largest risk. That is a complex step fraught with innumerable hazards, mainly because it takes up a long period of time on the island, where Nazis are swarming everywhere day and night."

"It makes the burden on the Danish Resistance the heaviest of all," he continued. "The voyages across the sea may also take a long time, but it would be most unusual for each fishing boat to run into more than one German patrol boat. On the other hand, every little step across Bornholm is an accident waiting to happen, as the breaking of a twig, the barking of a dog, the flurry of a scared chicken, a sneeze or a cough could all draw unwanted attention."

"So what are you driving at?" Dr. Levi said impatiently.

"I just want to paint the full picture of what to expect."

"Let him finish," Wolinski the lawyer urged. "We're not in a hurry to go home are we?"

"Because of all I've said," Kaminski continued, "I knew it would be crucial to get the Danish Resistance to help us, so I tackled the toughest job first."

"Good thinking," Levi said.

"I presented our dire need for escape as opposed to being gassed to death, as well as our plan of escape. To my great relief, the Danes were very interested!"

"Interested? What does that mean? What does that do for us?" Mark the plumber asked critically.

"Just a minute, let me finish." Kaminski went on, "Everything must start with an interest! If no interest, no sale. But fortunately they had great empathy for our people. They had plenty of their own in concentration camps in Germany and even some in Auschwitz."

"Really, Danes in Auschwitz?"

"Yes, I've heard of that," Levi answered.

"Well, anyway, the Danes agreed that the only thing we could do was to try to escape as soon as possible."

"But what did they think of our plan?"

"I'm coming to that. They thought it was highly risky and dangerous, but also very good and logical."

"Of course it's dangerous! This isn't just a game of cards!"

"But what else can we do?"

"I'm telling you they said the plan was good. They could suggest nothing better."

"So what else did they say??"

"Will they help us?"

"You know what they said?"

They said, "We'll do it!" Kaminski shouted and nearly fell off his chair with excitement.

"Shh!" They all whispered, "don't end the plan right here!"

"The walls have ears!" Levi warned.

"Fantastic," they all said quietly and shook hands.

"No one is more serious than the Danes and Norwegians when it comes to fighting the Nazis," Kaminski said.

"It's as though they actually rejoiced at the opportunity to put something over on them, as well as a chance to take revenge for their own suffering. I thought they might be very reluctant to take on the great risks involved, but you know what? They were actually ecstatic! Ecstatic, mind you! Have you ever heard of such a thing?"

"Great luck you've had, to meet with such fine people. How on earth did you manage that?"

"Well, I can't say too much about that," Kaminski whispered, "as you know, the walls have ears. But I have a business connection in Flensburg, a big city close to the Danish border, he speaks Danish, and he contacted the Danish Resistance right across the border, and they in turn spoke with Bornholm. The answer came back instantly by the same route."

"Thank God for your connection!"

"Yeah, you gotta know the right people."

"You got that right."

"Good work, Kaminski!" Levi said, "Now let's hear about the rest of the efforts."

"I was able to have a brief chat with a fellow plumber out in the city," Mark started. "I've known him for years. We trained together as apprentices, and he's OK, He's in the Polish Resistance, but hardly ever home, his wife said, too scared to be in one place for too long. He stays usually where he works, hops around a lot though."

"What did he say?"

"He said it could be done, but warned that we would have to take the shortest possible path to the coast; and never mind the usual fishing ports like Leba and Darlowo, they're too far away and too closely watched."

"Where can we go then?"

"He suggested Mielno, just six kilometers north of Koszalin, absolutely the quickest way!"

"But that's only a tiny place," Wolinski objected.

"Yeah, but that's why the Nazis have ignored it. Nobody ever goes there; so why should they go there? See?"

"OK, that makes sense."

"The tough part is crossing the land to get there. The terrain is pretty flat near the lake and the beach itself, but he said he knew a way."

"How?"

"There's an old path through the fields and between the sand dunes near the coast. There are many niches and hiding places along the path. No one ever goes there except in the summer."

"Can he get more help?"

"Yes, he's sure a couple of other guys will join as soon as we start."

"Why would they do that?"

"They've got nothing else to do right now!"

"Very well, your people can take charge of the trip from here to Mielno. I suspect we'll have to walk in order not to arouse suspicion."

"That's right! Cars on the small roads with lots of Jewish refugees would not look good."

"Now, Aron, what about you, can you supply us with the final link in the chain?" Levi asked.

"I can, but it's complicated, and I need to tell you all about it so you'll understand what we're up against. As a banker, I have connections in nearly every major city in Europe. I also have a friend in Vienna, a fellow banker, who does a lot of business with Sweden.

However, there is no telephone service here in the Ghetto, and no service out in the city to other countries except Germany, so I can't contact my friend in Vienna. Even if I could contact him, I am afraid the telephones have spies that listen in on all calls. The telegraph is of course not confidential, and the spies can read those easily. I had thought it might be possible for my friend in Vienna to send a messenger across the border to Switzerland to a contact in Zurich, who could then relay it to Sweden. As you know, Austria's western border sits like a footprint on Switzerland's eastern border." "But is it possible for someone to cross that border?" "Not legally, but a clever messenger could find a way to sneak across. But then again, the telephone spies might intercept such a call and our plan would be discovered," Aron elaborated.

"We know it's all difficult, and we understand what you can and cannot do and why, but tell us how you have succeeded. You said you could supply the last link in the plan, did you not?"

"Yes, yes, here is what I finally settled upon Since ordinary communication is either impossible or subject to discovery, and hand delivery is prohibitively slow, there remained only one possibility." "What's that?" they all asked leaning forward on their chairs.

"I asked Kaminski here to send my message to his contact in Flensburg who is able to reach the Danish Resistance, as you heard earlier. He was able not only to get the message out, but also to get an answer back, all by way of the Danish Resistance."

"What was the answer?" they all asked impatiently, "don't keep us in suspense!"

"Before I tell you, I need to mention something about the discussion that took place in Sweden."

"Wait a minute now, how come you're afraid to use the telephone because of spies, and yet Kaminski had no such problem giving his contact in Flensburg a message?" Mark asked.

"Yeah, how come?" Wolinski asked.

"Let me dispel your suspicions," Kaminski replied. "We simply communicated in a different language, one that Poles and Germans don't understand!"

"And what would that be?" Levi asked.

"Well, I didn't really want to reveal that, but since you ask, I'll whisper it just once, so listen closely."

"OK, OK."

"Portuguese!"

"You speak Portuguese?" Levi was astonished.

"Yes, my friend and I and a few friends from Denmark spent a delightful summer in Lisbon many years before the war and learned the language." Kaminski continued to whisper.

"How did you learn the language?"

"We made friends with some girls that spoke German, and they helped us a lot!"

"So you could call from Koszalin to Flensburg without difficulty?" Levi asked trying to eliminate any possibility of inconsistency, which might sink the whole project.

"Yes, I have a pass to visit my uncle out in the city. He is dying of TB. I called from there. When Aron asked me to do it one more time, it was easy to send a second message the same way."

"How did your friend relay it to Denmark?" Levi was relentless in picking the details apart, knowing that thousands of lives were at stake.

"The same way as before. He knew someone that spoke the same language."

"Was that one of the friends that spent the summer with you?"

"Yes"

"What luck," they all said.

"Now let me finish what I started to say before. Apparently the Swedes were not too happy about letting in what might be a huge number of refugees."

"Did they not want Jews?" Levi asked pointedly.

"No, no, that was not the issue; it was the sheer number that scared them a little."

"Just a little?"

"Yes, they didn't dwell on it very long."

"What then?"

"They were afraid of discovery and possible armed conflict. You know the Swedes have staunchly declined to take any sides in this war. They just want to preserve their peaceful existence." "We know, they have just sat out this war, letting every one else take a beating."

"Hey, let's not berate the Swedes for their decisions. I'm sure they realized that although they have the largest army and air force in Scandinavia, they'd be no match for the German War Machine, or "Wehrmacht" as they called it. The outcome of their intervention would not make any difference in the long run and would only cause more bloodshed." Levi instructed.

"Furthermore, Sweden is now able to provide a safe haven for thousands of persecuted people from several countries, and now for our people here. If they had been part of the warring factions, this life saving assistance would not be available to us. Did you guys even think of that?"

"You're always right, Levi," Aron said, "but look at all the Danes they let come across to Sweden. What's so different about our refugees?"

"Quite a lot." Levi answered, "The Danes are forming a secret liberation army in Sweden. It's growing daily. It'll return to kick the Nazis out and liberate Denmark very soon, once they're big enough."

"Wow, I didn't know that. Those Danes sure have guts!"

"Yeah."

"So how did the Swedes get over their fear of armed conflict?"

"The Danes convinced them."

"How?"

"The Danes with their humor! They said:

That's OK Sweden, we have a few knives, we'll take care of it!"

"Gads, where do they get that courage?" they all chuckled.

"Must be their Viking heritage!" Aron continued.

"So, the Swedes finally gave in. They realized that they were already accepting hundreds of Danes, and all was well with that program. To extend it to include Jewish refugees should not be too difficult."

"Hurray, we have a plan!"

"Let's get cracking. We have no time to lose.!" Levi became serious. "You all know you each have to figure out the details of your own section of the plan. The first refugees will need to leave the Ghetto as soon as the first fishing boat is ready to sail. I'll work with Mark here on the best way to leave the Ghetto.

It'll be soon, perhaps tomorrow night.

What fisherman was it you had spoken to, Mark?"

"I spoke to a Captain Jay. He's also in the Polish Resistance. He's ready now, weather permitting."

"OK, then plan for tomorrow night. Let's meet again in a week to discuss progress and problems."

They all left one at a time, just as they had arrived.

Chapter 5

The next day several loudspeakers were heard throughout the Ghetto, and all activity and work stopped. The harsh voice of a German soldier was so loud it was unclear; but one phrase was repeated over and over again:

"Wir müssen alle Juden schneller abführen."

"What are they saying?" A little boy asked.

"They are saying they must lead all Jews away faster."

"So what does that mean?

"It means they'll send more of us to the camps every day. We'll have much less time here in the Ghetto."

"Is that good?"

"No, it's not good, but don't you worry, we'll find a better way."

Mark had heard the announcements. He knew time was running out. He made a plan for getting people out of the Ghetto starting the next day, as desired by Dr. Levi, and went to his house to present it to the group.

"There're several ways to get our people out of the Ghetto," he began, "one more cryptic than the other. Sooner or later they'd all arouse suspicion. Already we'll arouse suspicion by the increasing number of people that'll be missing from the Ghetto; and that'll have to be downplayed as best we can. We don't need a cloak and dagger type of plan like we first envisioned. We'll use a more realistic plan, one that's based on simple common sense. It may be more risky, but it'll be a lot more practical."

"What's that?"

"It's the red and black pass. It was conceived as a way to keep our people inside the Ghetto. We'll turn it around and use it as a means of getting them out!"

"I like your way of thinking. The Nazis think they're so smart; little do they know they're in many ways rather stupid," the business man added.

"Quite so! It's because they're narrow minded and focused only on their evil ideas and how to perpetrate them. When it comes down to constructive thinking, they're virtually devoid of any brain power," Dr. Levi piped in.

"According to the Nazis," Mark continued, "some of the people have a legitimate reason for going in and out of the Ghetto on a daily basis. They're doing so repeatedly by means of this small card with their name, sex and birthday stamped on it. They have business out in the city, to care for a sick relative, or to work at a place useful to the Nazis, such as small craftsmen, shoemakers, plumbers, carpenters, auto mechanics, etc.

They have no picture or detailed description of the person like a passport. The guards didn't want to be burdened with lengthy inspections of papers; they just wanted a yes or no type item. The little red and black card could just be waved in the air in order to be recognized, very quick and efficient. And that's exactly what we need. Such a card will allow that same quick and efficient exit for our people."

"Then they won't be leaving the Ghetto at midnight?"

"No, there's no need for that. They'll all leave late in the afternoon at random intervals, ten to fifteen minutes apart, so as not to give the impression of being a group. Once outside, they'll make their way to Darlowo, where they'll be hidden in the old castle by the river Wieprza. It dates back to when the Vikings occupied Poland's north shore."

"Are you serious? That place is guarded day and night!"

"Yes, but after 6:00 O'clock there's only one guard in the front at the main gate. He walks back and forth over a 200 foot distance along the entire front of the castle. It seems rather silly, but it'll allow us to sneak by him easily during the five minutes each time his back is turned."

"How'll the people get into the castle, and then where'll they go?"

"The guards have a small room just inside the main gate where they hang out during the day. There's nobody there at night, except this one guard. He comes out front through a small door in the big main gate, which he closes but doesn't lock, in case he needs to rush inside to protect himself or call for help. That's the door that the people will use to quickly and quietly get inside. Remember, no one ever goes there at night. There're no utilities at the castle. No restroom, no lights, no water, no heat, no furnishings. No nothing. It's completely bare. Everything of value has been stripped out by the Nazis, and everything of no value has been thrown out and used as firewood by the townspeople. The castle is completely empty, and no one goes there, except a rare school excursion in the spring."

"Are you sure the guard wouldn't detect anything?"

"Absolutely! The guard does not expect anyone, so he's not very alert. Can you imagine staring intently out in the darkness, hoping to find something unusual, night after night, and never finding anything? It would drive you crazy. The guard knows that, and he may even take a nap later in the evening, slouched in a chair in his little room; then of course he locks the door. So the people have to get inside early on, right after he comes on duty, while the door's still unlocked."

"OK, so where do they go once inside the gate? Is there not a big open courtyard?"

"Yes, that's too open for them to traverse, and the castle doors are of course locked. Here's the thing!

They'll simply go into the guard's room! On the inside wall there's a door that opens into a hallway that runs down towards the river. It then turns abruptly to the right, going parallel to the river a hundred feet or so, finally opening into a large hall at the northwest corner of the castle."

"They do all that in darkness?"

"Yes, but they'll have a small bicycle lantern with a weak light that'll be shaded to avoid detection."

"Then what?"

"Is that a meeting hall or what?"

"Probably. It could also have been storage for lots of goods or foods. I don't know. A few steps to the left, as you enter from the long hallway, there's a secret passage down to the river."

"A secret passage? Maybe the Nazis know about it already."

"I seriously doubt it. Hardly anyone knows about it. I have never heard it mentioned, even before the war."

"How did you find it then?"

"Oh, I get around," Mark continued. "Castles have always intrigued me. They're a piece of history, a witness to a bygone era of the wealth and power of a few fortunate aristocrats. They had the time to think of everything. Much like we have all the mechanical toys, some to play with, others to cook with, many to work with. So they had passages, secret doors, gates, weapons, primitive tools, and some very ingenious inventions, long since forgotten. However, we're fortunate to be able to make use of some of all that, as long as we know about them."

"I never knew you were such a historian, Mark," the lawyer remarked.

"Yeah, well, anyway, in the thick stone wall, four steps to the left of the entrance, there's a small three by five foot section that pivots near one side, allowing a person to squeeze through to a stairway going down to a short hallway, opening into a smaller hall right next to the river. There's actually a large cutout in the floor, so the river comes right into the hall."

"Is there some sort of gate to the river outside?"

They were all fascinated by Mark's past explorations.

"Yes, there's a large wooden gate, much like those in a fire station, 18 feet high and 18 feet wide, divided in the middle, so the doors can swing open. It'll allow a boat to enter and come right into the hall!"

"Sounds fantastic! How did you ever find that?" Asked Levi.

"I've known about it for many years. It just has never been of any importance to me until now."

"That really sounds exciting. The people can then board a fishing boat in the quiet darkness of the hall by the river and leave through the gate when ready. Is that your plan?"

"That's right!"

"What I like is that it sounds quite practical, but what about noise from the boat; wouldn't the guard hear that?"

"We'll insulate the engine compartment on the boat as best we can, so the noise can't be heard very far. Also the guard is actually on the other side of the castle, quite a ways away. I doubt he could hear anything."

"OK, it all sounds good, but how'll the people get from Koszalin all the way to Darlowo? That's no less than 40 km! It would be a very a long walk!!"

"I know it sounds like a lot, but you know, even though the 6 km to Mielno seems a lot less, that short distance is still terribly long, when you have to walk it. Our people are not athletes; they're poorly nourished and tired. They just can't walk that far."

"Are you saying they can't even walk to Mielno?"

"Yes, and besides, the landscape is rather flat and open by the lake and more so near the coast. That makes it more difficult to stay out of sight; even a single person would stand out more."

"Then what can we do?"

"I've decided that the most inconspicuous way to travel would be the natural way that everybody does. Take the bus!"

"Are you crazy? What if the bus is stopped and inspected, the refugees would be discovered at once!"

"No one has ever stopped a bus and demanded it be inspected. Furthermore, the refugees will go unnoticed as they mingle with the large after work crowd taking the bus."

"What happens when the bus gets into Darlowo? Where'll they go then?"

"It stops close to the castle. As people get off, the refugees will scatter with the others and gradually work themselves back around to the castle grounds, as darkness falls over the area. There're no street lights there, and the darkness will easily hide the people."

"Yeah, but some people might stand out by their, their…"

"Lack of 'sneaking' ability?" Mark felt compelled to complete the thought.

"Yes, yes, that's it; they don't know how to be a thief in the night."

"No, but I'll show them."

"So, you've been a thief in the night, Mark?"

"No, but I've known a few as a kid."

"Still sounds risky to me."

"I'm open to suggestions."

There were a few moments of silence, but no-one came forth with a better plan, or any plan at all.

"Well, eh…it's not that there might be a better way to go, but whether your plan will work at all!"

"Even if there's no better way, we must not throw caution to the wind."

"The whole escape program could be blown to pieces," Levi interrupted with his usual unwavering logic.

"I realize all that, but it's a plan that we're able to put into action; and of course it'll take some effort.

Preparation beforehand, courage and alertness as we go, and finally stubbornness to hang in there till it's finished. Our people are not stupid.

They know the score. They know what's at stake.

They can be shown what they don't already know; I'm convinced of that, and I know we can succeed! How long I don't know.

All I know for certain is that we'll keep on trying till there's no one left to rescue!"

"With such determination, how can we not proceed?"

"How can we not succeed?" Levi drew a long sigh.

"Let's get on with it!"

CHAPTER 6

Mark wasted no time.

After leaving Levi's house, he went directly to his neighbor, a small family of five. They were a young couple with two young children and their grandfather.

As with most people in the Ghetto, they had lost their home, livelihood and goods, in fact everything except the clothes on their backs.

Their lives were not only on hold; their lives were over.

They didn't know they were doomed; only a miracle could save them. He chose them as the first to go. For them that was their miracle.

He knocked softly on their door.

The husband opened the door a crack.

"Who's there?" He asked, as though he preferred not to know.

"It's me, Mark, from next door. May I come in?"

"Yes, of course. Please excuse my precaution. You never know who may come at this time."

"I know, it's late, an hour after curfew, but I've got something urgent to discuss."

"What could that be, more bad news for us?"

"No, no, this is good news."

"Good," he breathed a sigh of relief," come in and sit down. I'll call my wife."

They sat down at the dining table. The rest of the family had gone to bed.

"Tell us now, what can be good news?" They asked.

"Actually, I have both bad and good news. The good news'll wipe out the bad, I promise you, so don't be frightened. Can you promise me that?"

"We'll try."

"Then you must hear me out," Mark continued.

"All of us here in the Ghetto are being sent to a camp in Southern Poland called Auschwitz."

"Yes we've heard. There we can finally start a new life."

"No, it's not a new life. It's a death camp. Everyone going there is killed by poison gas, sometimes the day they arrive."

"No! But it can't be!" They both said with horrified expressions.

"Yes, but we have a plan to escape from the Ghetto and flee to safety across the Baltic to Sweden."

"But how?"

"Who is 'We'?"

"That's a long story, and I can only tell you a few things. A group of us have learned of these things and have worked hard to arrange a plan to lead you all to safety. Now, you must leave here tomorrow afternoon at 4:15."

"So soon?"

"We just couldn't leave tomorrow!"

"Yes we can, dear; we must"

"It's 'Do or Die'," Mark said with a serious tone. "Here's a pass for each person. You must leave only one at a time, ten minutes apart and get on the bus to Darlowo. Each of you'll take one of the children along with you."

"What do we do at Darlowo?"

"The bus stops near the castle after dark. You'll all get off the bus with other people at the castle. Then you'll take separate paths to the castle grounds, where I'll meet you. You must not enter the castle grounds before dark. That's very important. You must be aware of other people around you, walk naturally, and only head for the castle grounds when you're alone on the street. Do you understand?"

"Yes, yes."

"You must never run away. If stopped by anyone, say you've been visiting a sick aunt over in number 26 River Street and are getting some fresh air. Is that clear?"

"Yes, yes, but how'll we find you?"

"There are some tall bushes near the street as you first come to the castle grounds. They grow all the way up to the main gate. I'll be right behind them down by the street."

"What then?" They were all questions.

"I'll lead you to a fishing boat that'll take you to safety in Denmark. From there you'll journey to Sweden." Mark was careful not to reveal too much.

"Don't tell a soul, and don't go out! Leave quietly and casually at 4:15. Don't miss the bus!"

"This is so sudden. There's so much we need to ask. There's so much we need to do. What can we bring?"

"I know, I know, but your lives are at stake. You'll learn as you go. You'll escape tomorrow! You can't bring anything except the clothes you're wearing and these passes that'll get you out of the Ghetto. Good night."

"Good night and thank you for helping us."

As Mark quietly slipped out the door, the husband and wife looked fearfully at each other.

They were speechless.

They sat down again.

They hugged each other tightly.

"It's the only way," he said.

"I know," she whispered tearfully.

CHAPTER 7

It was 4:15.

The husband and his nine year old son walked out the door. Two girls were playing on the sidewalk across the street. Father and son casually walked toward the gate in the tall fence. The guard was just looking at the pass of an incoming gentleman with a briefcase. He was just about to open the man's briefcase when he looked up and spotted the two people heading toward him. He stared at them for a moment, and his eye caught the red and black passes they were waving at him. He nodded and waved them on by.

The first two refugees had left the Ghetto.

They turned the corner and headed for a little park where they would wait for the bus.

At 4:30 the grandfather left the house and made his way down the street toward the gate, walked up to the guard, showed him his pass and was led out through the gate. At 4:45 the wife and seven year old daughter left the house, and showed their passes to the guard, then let through the gate. Close to 5 o'clock, the little family approached the bus stop from several directions to avoid looking like a group.

At exactly at 5 o'clock the Darlowo bus appeared. It was nearly full with all types of people just getting off work down town and going back home to the beach cities. The few scattered remaining seats were soon taken by the family.

The sun set behind a large formation of low clouds over Koszalin, causing a magnificent display of red and gold light with long sharp rays of white striking the city.

"Look at all the red clouds," the daughter said.

"Fantastic. I'll bet you'll never see that again," the father said.

He realized that this was the last time they would ever see Koszalin.

The bus stopped briefly to let off a few riders at the small town of Bukowo, little more than half way to Darlowo. Soon it would be dark. A half hour later, as the bus pulled into Darlowo, the town was in complete darkness. The sunset curfew did not permit any lights to be visible. This was mainly to protect against air raids, when any light could be a target. It also discouraged people from being outside after sunset.

Once off the bus, people scattered in all directions, and so did the little family. The men went one way, and the women went a slightly different way. They soon found the corner with the bushes, arriving a few minutes apart as directed. Just then, a dark figure stepped out from behind the bushes.

Their hearts stopped.

They held their breath.

Was this the end?

"Hello, I'm glad you made it!" The figure said.

"Oh, it's you! What a relief!"

"Any problems on the way?" Mark asked.

"Not a one."

"Come, let's quickly go behind this row of bushes. No talking, and watch your step. Don't step on any branches. When I cross the grounds to the gate, just follow me as quickly and quietly as you can."

"OK."

Mark waited till the guard had turned around and started to walk away, then looked all around to be sure no one else was coming. He beckoned the others to follow. They all moved quietly across the dirt road that surrounded the castle and ducked in through the little door in the gate.

The guard was only half way toward the end of the castle wall, oblivious to anything happening behind him. Mark continued to lead the family into the hallway along the river, finally stopping in the big hall.

"Let's just rest here a moment," he said. "We're about to go down a stairway that leads into a lower hall that has a large opening in the floor, where the river comes up near the level of the floor. You must not make a sound, because sound carries quite far over water. The hall will be like an echo chamber, and any noise will be greatly magnified. So, not a sound! We'll wait there for our boat, which may already be there. Ready to go?"

"Yes."

"Give me a hand," Mark said.

The husband followed Mark over to the secret door where they struggled to turn the heavy section of wall so it would open and allow a person to squeeze into the stairway. They all entered, and Mark entered last in order to close the wall behind them.

Their steps echoed loudly through the stairway as they approached the lower hall.

"Quiet!" Mark whispered, "Remember, any noise gets magnified in here."

The hall was cold, as the cold waters of the Baltic Sea was driven up the Weiprza River and into the hall, eagerly lapping the sides of the floor. As they entered the hall, they were all shocked.

"There's a boat in here!" the boy whispered loudly, his eyes wide from surprise.

Captain Jay was right on time. He had silently drifted close to the castle, as he let the wind push him in. A few thrusts of the engine, and he ducked into the short channel, slid through the gates in front of the hall, and moored right against the floor.

"Great to see you, Jay."

"Great to see you too, Mark. Let's get the people aboard and secured."

"Come aboard," Mark waived the family over. "You will now need to lie down in a space under the floor. It's padded, but not as good as a real bed. You'll need to stay quiet for the next four hours until we can safely let you up again in Denmark. I know it's not very comfortable, but this is what'll save your lives, just remember that! If at any time you feel you must get out, remember you may go right into your immediate death, if the Nazis are anywhere nearby."

With those somber reminders, the family quickly squeezed themselves one by one into the small space under the floor. As the cover was put in place and locked with another board, the grandfather was heard saying "As close as we are in here it's a good thing we're all friends!"

The hiding place was now virtually undetectable. As soon as it was covered, the fishermen retrieved the mooring line holding the boat against the floor of the hall. The crew pushed the gates closed, as Captain Jay gave just a slight push with the engine to ease the boat out into the river. Under the veil of darkness, the current silently carried the boat out to sea.

Mark hitched a ride with the boat and jumped off on the pier of the little fishing harbor, near the mouth of the river. Captain Jay picked up a little speed going into the light onshore breeze and headed toward the Danish island of Bornholm. He looked at his two trusted crew members and smiled.

"Here we go!" He whispered.

Only one thing would stand between Captain Jay and the island of Bornholm. A German patrol boat!

Could they avoid being boarded?

Time would tell.

CHAPTER 8

It was 7 O'clock.

Captain Jay had brought the first five refugees safely to Denmark. The interception by a Nazi patrol boat had been unavoidable, but fortunately he'd managed to weather that crisis unscathed. His precious cargo of a family of refugees was now in the hands of the Danish Resistance. With great relief he pointed the bow of his fishing boat back south toward the little harbor of Darlowo.

The sun peaked above the calm sea, throwing a handful of golden red beams of light in all directions. A few wild swans hurried across the sun, trying to catch up with their flock migrating south. As the island of Bornholm vanished into the early morning mist, Jay was free to relax and reflect on his present situation.

I've done my job.

I've survived a Nazi boarding patrol.

I've eluded other Nazi vessels.

You never know when the next encounter will come.

You never know what it'll bring.

You never know if you'll live to tell about it.

You know it'll come out of nowhere.

Man, it's been a tense night

What kind of life is that?

Not exactly what I always dream about.

But for now, I have a mission to accomplish.

A mission of mercy.

A mission to save hundreds of innocent lives.

Men, women and children, all civilians.

So far, so good. But it's only just begun.

A light breeze began to blow as Captain Jay advanced further South out in the open waters of the Baltic. There were no other boats in sight, and Jay pushed the throttle to full speed ahead. The little boat leaped across the small waves, as if it knew it was going home.

The cool breeze on his face was a delightful massage, relaxing all the tension of the night.

What a beautiful morning!

His thoughts turned to the plans for the day.

First to get home; then to sleep.

He felt great just thinking about that.

Then after supper, back to the boat.

Back to the castle.

There to pick up another group of refugees.

What would they be like?

I hope they're as good as this group was.

They were quiet as church mice.

They knew the score.

They wanted to live.

They were survivors.

I hope they'll all be like that.

His thoughts were suddenly interrupted by one of his crew poking a sleepy head out of the locker.

"Are we there yet?" He mused.

"Oh, shut up! This weather is great, and the sea is quiet. We're going to stay out here forever!

"OK with me!"

The sleepy head retracted itself back into the locker. With his eyes on the horizon, Jay resumed his daydreaming.

I never realized I was so much at home on the sea. To be one with nature is absolutely the most calming experience you'll ever have. And it's like the serenity of nature is so irresistible, that once you experience it, you're addicted for life. Wherever you are, you'll always long for it, and you'll always want to return to it.

Jay kept on day dreaming.

He would be home soon enough.

On the shore at Darlowo, Mark made his way toward a friend's house on 26 River Street, a little ways from the harbor.

"What brings you out here to Darlowo?" His friend asked.

"Oh, I just thought I'd see if there was any work to be found out here."

"You know there's less work here than in Koszalin."

"I know, but every little bit helps."

"You can come along with me," his friend said, "I can always use good help."

"Thank you so much."

"I know you like to stay close to your work, so you can stay at my house, if you like."

"That's very kind of you; I'd really like that.

"Just don't think we have lots of big construction jobs out here; we have only little jobs!"

"No problem, I assure you."

Mark realized that at this point with all the planning and arranging over with, his role in the escape plan was reduced to one hour every night after sunset, when he met and guided the refugees from the street through the castle to the fishing boat.

He began to think about how he could keep doing that, once he had worn out his welcome at his friend's house.

Well, I'll cross that bridge when I come to it, he thought.

He also realized that he could not reveal his part in the rescue operation to anyone, not even to a good friend. One slip of the tongue to the wrong person, and all hell could break loose.

Back in the Ghetto, Dr. Levi was on the edge of his seat.

"I still haven't heard a thing about the escape," he said to Rebecca.

"You know it'll be at least several days before you can even hope to hear anything!"

"I suppose you're right."

"Sometimes no news is good news!"

"Right again!"

"I'm sure if any part of the plan had failed, there would be lots of rumors flying by now."

"That's probably true. It's just that I hate being kept in suspense."

"Don't we all?"

"I've made a waiting list of small groups of people that'll leave together. Each group'll be assigned a specific day on which to leave. If any problems develop causing cancellation, it'll be up to either Mark or Captain Jay to get word back to me. So, not having heard any such word as yet, I'll go ahead and notify the next group to leave.

The second group to go was another family of five next door to the Levis. There was a husband and wife, two children and an aunt who lived a few houses down the street. Dr. Levi went next door to tell them the good news. He didn't want to scare them, but he had to knock on their door. But this would be a different kind of a knock. It was definitely not a thunderous pounding; it was a soft and friendly knock.

The door was opened a crack, and an anxious eye peered out through the crack.

"Don't be afraid," Levi said hastily, "it's just me, your neighbor next door."

"What a relief!"

"I really understand your fear of anyone knocking on your door; but believe me, I do have something important to tell you, if you'll let me in for just a moment."

"Yes, yes, come in."

"I'm sure you've heard that many families are awakened just before sunrise by the shock of loud banging on their doors. The Nazis call them out of bed and herd them outside into the waiting train to Auschwitz.

"Is that what's happening?"

"Yes, and they're forced to hastily grab their clothes and any item within reach such as a picture or a book. They join others huddled together, standing room only. There're no seats in the cattle cars!"

"Yes we've heard that, but what is it you can tell us"

"In spite of all that terrible news, I do have some very good news for you! You'll be able to leave this Ghetto already this afternoon and travel to safety in Denmark and Sweden."

"Fantastic! When do we leave?"

"There are some risks involved."

"We don't care! We'll go right now!"

It was nearly 11 o'clock. They would bring Aunt Emma over to them and get ready to leave by 4:15.

At 11 o'clock they heard a loud whistle. They hurried over to

47

the window and watched in horror as the fully loaded train to Auschwitz slowly began to pull out of the Ghetto with nearly 200 poor souls, whose lives would soon be snuffed out by poison gas. None of them would know until the very end; and even then, some would never know.

Suddenly their eyes caught a familiar figure leaning out from the back of the train.

"There's Aunt Emma!"

"Oh no!"

"She can't go on the train! She's got to go with us!"

They started to run down the stairs toward the front door to stop the train. They wanted to take Aunt Emma off the train.

In the last second, the husband grabbed his wife on the front steps and held her back.

"Wait a minute," he said "we can't do that."

"We've got to!"

"We can't! It won't do any good. They won't stop the train. They won't let us take Emma off the train. They might even put us on the train! We can't fight them. It's useless." Heartbroken they returned to the window.

"Had we only told her sooner she would be here now."

"Yes, but we couldn't do that. We didn't know ourselves, until a minute ago."

"To come so close, and then to lose. It's just not fair!"

"No it's not, but you know the world has never been a fair place."

They all stared in silence as the end of the last car, with aunt Emma still looking back, slowly moved out of the gate and vanished.

"How awful for her!"

"What must she think of us?"

"I'm sure she wonders if we simply abandoned her."

"I'll never be able to forget the image of Emma looking back from the train. She looked so lost, so terribly sad."

"It's a picture that'll stay with us forever."

They started to cry.

They cried for the people on the train.

They cried for Aunt Emma.

They cried for themselves.

"A miracle has come our way."

"We're going to be spared."

"We've been touched by the hand of God."

"But for the Grace of God, there go we!"

Overcome with emotion, they could not eat.

They all sat down in silence for a while. Finally they got up and prepared for their new lives.

CHAPTER 9

After landing on Bornholm, the little group of refugees was quickly led in under the cover of nearby bushes by a member of the Danish Resistance.

"Hi, my name is Hans. Welcome to Bornholm. You're now on Danish soil, and I'll be your guide to bring you across the island to a small fishing village called Tejn. There you'll be able to get on a small fishing boat going to Sweden."

"Just what we need, another sardine can trip!" The father tried to be funny.

"Let's all sit down a few minutes," Hans said. "I know it's been hard on you to travel this way, but I don't think you would like to stay in Denmark right now. We have too many Nazis here, maybe even more than in Poland. They're swarming everywhere."

"No, no, I was just joking, we'll be happy to go to Sweden in any way possible."

"OK then, let me just tell you what to expect during your trip across Bornholm.

We Danes are born on bicycles, and everybody rides them. We'll also ride them in two groups of three.

One group'll be husband and wife with son, the other grandfather, daughter and myself. I've brought some colorful clothes for you, so you'll look more like Danes.

There'll be no talking or laughing. I'll show you where and when to stop to eat and rest. We should be in Tejn this evening after dark. There's no time to waste in getting you off the island again, so you'll have to leave on the fishing boat as soon as this evening. OK?

I've brought some food. Would you like a nice Danish breakfast of rolls, French bread and Danish pastry?"

"Oh boy! Would we ever."

"In that case we better rest a little while before we start," Hans continued. "After your strenuous night in tight quarters, you'll need some rest before the long journey to Tejn."

Two hours later, as a red sun seemed to pull itself up out of the Baltic Sea, the six bikes got silently underway. They took a small road from the seashore that could barely accommodate a single car driving on it, but there was plenty of room for the bikes. After a while, the road merged with the main road leading to the center of the island. Before going that way, it was time for a quick rest; and Hans led the group to a small church with an attached four winged farm, where they could hide for a short while. Hans knew the owner and could use his farm as a stopover.

As they came to the end of the long driveway, lined on both sides by tall Poplar trees, typical of all Danish farms, a German patrol in an open car came down the highway.

Could they have been spotted?

"Oh, oh, the car is slowing down by the driveway."

"They're coming this way!" Hans warned."Get in the barn."

They scrambled though the main portal into the square courtyard, flanked on all sides by barns. They dashed across the yard into the far barn door, threw the bikes into the back corner and buried them quickly under piles of hay, then crawled under the hay themselves.

The German car was now entering the courtyard in a brazen breach of privacy, immediately drawing the owner out of the back door into the courtyard. Pigs were snorting and squealing, chickens flurried about squawking, and a few horses whinnied in agreement.

"What's the meaning of this?" He scolded. "We do have a front door, you know!"

"Good day, Sir," said the Nazi officer riding in the back seat like a general.

"Have you seen any strangers around," the officer continued.

"Strangers? We don't see many people out here; we only see people we know."

"OK then, can we take a look around?"

"Yes, we have two pigs in there; they would like to meet you," he pointed to the open door where Hans and his group were hiding. "Over there, a couple of horses."

The Nazi officer got out of the car and went directly to the open barn door, like it was left open just for him. He looked around at all the piles of hay and heard a few noises to the left.

"That's the pigs starting to complain about the food," the owner said.

The Nazi walked a few steps to the left, peeked over a small wooden wall, and got a whiff of two huge pigs. He quickly turned around and faced the large pile of hay in the corner.

He drew his pistol.

"Anybody hiding in there?" He asked, pointing his pistol at the pile of hay.

"No, no, that's what the horses eat. Have you ever been on a farm?"

The owner tried to divert the Nazi's attention.

"No, never," he said, clearly not interested in life on a farm.

"What if I were to fire a couple of shots in there?"

The officer continued as he scrutinized the owner's face for any sign of nervousness.

"You're just dying to shoot at the hay aren't you?! Well, ha, ha," the owner chuckled, "I would have to tell the Kommandant that one of his officers is so scared these days, that he even shoots at piles of hay! Ha, ha, ha. He would laugh at that, I'm sure!"

"Shut up! That's not funny."

The officer was clearly embarrassed.

"Not a word to anyone, you understand?"

"All right, all right."

The officer returned his pistol to its holster and then indignantly stepped into the patrol car and motioned to his driver to leave. He waved a silent goodbye. The owner strained hard not to burst out laughing, as the car turned out of the portal and sped out the driveway.

Hans emerged from the hay and greeted the owner.

"Again you shall have my thanks," he began.

"Ah, don't mention it. I needed a little joke to start the day."

"I'm glad it turned into that!"

"You know, as serious as these times are, there's always room for a little humor. It makes life a little easier. In fact, it's the only thing that makes it tolerable! Don't you think?"

"Yeah, especially when the joke's on them," Hans shook his head in the direction of the fast parting Nazis.

"Of course, they make such good subjects!"

"Thanks again," Hans said as he shook hands with the owner and beckoned the cautiously appearing group to come further out and get going.

Somewhat shaken by a second close call in the last 24 hours, the group started to ride faster, making the physical exercise repress their anxiety and hunger. They were soon near the central and scenic part of the island.

"I'm afraid we'll have to hurry on past the tourist attractions, since there may be Nazis having lunch in these parts," Hans warned the group. "As you can see, this area is more populated; people on bikes, buses, even horseback and buckboards, and also some just hiking through the forests."

A German patrol car went by, not paying much attention to the various people on the road. Suddenly Hans made a sharp left turn; the rest quickly followed.

"This is a small country road leading all the way to Tejn," Hans continued. "It runs parallel to the ocean ten kilometers inland. It's nearly deserted as opposed to the faster coast highway, taken by most people, including the Germans. Over to the right just a few miles is an ancient 'Round Church' dating back many centuries. It's the hallmark of this island, because there's none like it in the whole world. It looks like a fortress, as many of the ancient churches do, since people could always seek refuge in the churches. In those times most warriors respected religious beliefs. It should not surprise you that the Nazis do not. So don't seek refuge from the Nazis in a church. Most likely, that Round Church was also an observatory. People have long been fascinated by astronomy and its earlier cousin astrology."

"I've heard this church is very special in some way, is that correct?"

"Yes, it's been mentioned in some ancient biblical writings, as belonging to a group of churches linked to the early days of Christianity. Some day you may wish to return for a visit to all these sights, but for now, just keep on riding!"

Toward early evening, a car engine was heard far behind them. They all went off the road immediately and hid behind a patch of high bushes. As they watched the road, a man in a brown coat on a bike peddled past them as fast as he could, obviously fleeing from somebody. Soon three Nazis with guns drawn roared by at full speed, followed a minute later by the sound of gun fire and squealing brakes.

"Damn!" Hans whispered. "That may have been one of ours."

"Let's go see if we can help him," said the wife.

"No, we can't do that,"

"Why not?"

"We don't dare show ourselves. You see, we've all been raised to come to the aid of anyone whose life is in danger, but you must realize we are at war here, and the rules are different. If we rush in to help someone, we may wind up with six bullets in the chest. It may seem selfish not to risk your own life to save another life, or to save someone from the enemy. But you must also realize that if you get shot in the process, you can't be of much help to that person. You have risked your life against overwhelming odds. You could be of much better help if you wait till it's safer. You must assess the situation and surroundings before you rush in to help."

"Why don't we all hide, and you could go alone to try and help?"

"Yes, it's a nice thought, but not only would I risk my life, I would also risk all of yours."

"Why is that?"

"I am your guide and protector. My first obligation is to all of you as a group, as well as individuals. It is the principle of saving many versus saving one or a few.

That's always a tough dilemma, and many movies have featured that mental conflict. It must be decided by the circumstances, which have to be very favorable

55

for someone to risk the lives of many to save a few or any one person. In war, danger has a way of always escalating when you least expect it. It may do so in peacetime also, but then you don't always have someone shooting at you."

"How do we get past them?" The husband asked.

"We'll wait right here till it's dark; then we'll sneak by them."

At that very moment, the patrol car returned at a slower speed, the Nazis having completed their murder mission. Hans and his group safely mounted their bikes and continued quickly in the opposite direction toward the North coast.

"We don't dare stop to look for an injured person. If the Nazis have left the scene, that person is most likely dead. They'll be on the lookout for his friends, like us, to come out searching for him. They would then surprise us all. No, there's no stopping now until we reach Tejn."

Soon Hans made a right turn toward the coast; the others followed close by, and Hans played travel guide.

"Tejn is a small village on the rocky North coast of Bornholm, that a few fishing vessels have called home for decades. A small number of artists live here too, and literally give the village a bit of color. The Germans come there only when passing through to the South-Eastern corner of the island. As compared to the popular beach towns of Allinge and Sandvig up the coast, Tejn is the little town that time forgot. Fortunately it's also the little town that the Germans forgot, at least for now. They might soon come to curse its existence."

The sun had set before they arrived in Tejn, and the island was shrouded in darkness. Very few lights could still be seen in the little village, because of the sunset curfew.

"We'll go off the main road here," Hans said as he led his group into a series of side streets.

"Here we'll avoid any stray German soldiers who might be

roaming around. We're coming down to the little harbor, and look out there, you can see a boat drifting two miles out in the ocean, raking in its nets and preparing to come into the harbor with its catch of fish.

But between you and me, it's not just getting in its catch of the day, it's also keeping a very watchful eye on traffic out at sea, ready to warn us of any Nazi patrols coming this way."

"Is that our private ferry to Sweden?" The man asked, pointing to the only boat in the harbor.

"I hope so," Hans replied, "it's moored with its stern toward town, to hide all action taking place in front of the wheelhouse."

Hans knocked softly on the side of the boat.

"I've been expecting you, Hans," a bearded face said as it popped up over the railing. You're right on time. I like that."

"Hi there Nils, I didn't know you were sleeping on deck. Yeah, I try to be on time, but sometimes things happen on the way that snatch your time away, you know."

"Don't tell me you had some trouble on the way?"

"Yes, we were hiding in a barn when this wannabe general, came by in an open car."

"Oh, how did you elude him?"

"The owner made a fool out of him, so he stopped his war games and left."

"Do say! That was neat."

"I know! Then later on we saw a chase on the old country road, right past 'Virgin Hill'. I think someone got shot and probably killed. I couldn't stop to see."

"No of course. Well, you're here in one piece, and so are your people! Get them aboard so we can leave. It makes me nervous to have so many people in one place."

Nils wasted no time getting the people out of sight. He showed them the same type of hiding place as they had night before. They all crawled in.

"This one is slightly padded, but still a shallow compartment. Fortunately it won't be as long a trip as last night," Nils assured them, "but the sea might be rough, and I'll be going fast."

He closed the cover, and his only crew member cast off. The fishing boat left the harbor at a fair speed, since there were no other boats around for miles.

Soon the fishing boat was leaping across the waves toward Sweden.

"You think we'll meet any patrols out there tonight?" His crew asked.

"No, I hope to avoid any encounters by crossing before any patrols show up. The waters we'll travel are right on the outskirts of where the Nazis would go, so they're not usually out here early in the evening, but might get this far out later on. I think we can feel fairly safe at this time. As you know, the shorter route to Sweden from Bornholm is to the town of Ystad on the South Coast; but it's also a busy ferry route, so I'm going to take a path far to the east of that. I'm aiming for a place called "Skillinge", just north of the South-East corner of Sweden."

Soon they were in lee of the point. North beyond that, the seas became calm and scattered lights began to appear on the fast approaching shoreline.

"It's always nice to get in lee of the land as soon as possible at the end of a voyage. And doesn't it make you feel good to be "almost" there?"

"Yeah, it does, and somehow I feel safer in the lee of that point back there."

"Exactly, and we're clearly well beyond that now.

Once beyond that point, we're definitely in protected Swedish waters, where no German patrol boat will dare go."

Nils tied up at a small pier in Skillinge, and five happy refugees scrambled up and out of the hiding place and set their shaky feet on dry land. They were now in Sweden, where they were met by a family who brought them to their home for the night.

"Back to Bornholm!" Nils shouted as he pointed the bow out to sea.

CHAPTER 10

It was four O'clock in the afternoon.

There was a knock on the door.

Dr. Levi and his wife looked at each other with surprise and suspicion. They weren't expecting anyone.

Unexpected visitors were usually harbingers of trouble, and doors were not opened for them.

The knock was heard again. This time it was softer.

"I'm going to peek out the window between the curtains and see if there are any signs of Nazis out there," Dr Levi said quietly. "The bus from Szczecin just left the bus stop. I don't see any Gestapo cars outside. It might just be a friendly visitor," he continued, as he went over to the door and listened for a moment.

"Who's there?" He asked.

"It's me, Rachel!" A young woman's voice answered.

Levi opened the door wide and greeted his daughter with a big hug.

"Why Rachel, what brings you here so unexpectedly?"

"It's a long story. I'll tell you inside. I need to sit down."

"Yes, of course, come over to the sofa."

"Thanks"

Rachel plopped herself down in the corner of a monstrous sofa that almost swallowed her completely.

"Oh, that feels so good!"

"Rachel!" Her mother appeared and leaned over and kissed her. "Don't get up. Just relax. Tell us what's going on with you."

The Levis sat down by Rachel, Joseph on a chair close by and her mother next to her on the sofa.

Rachel continued in a distraught voice.

"They came this morning.

They woke me up at five O'clock in the morning, almost breaking the door down.

They barely gave me time to put my clothes on.

They treated me like a common criminal.

They said they found out that I was Jewish, and that now I had to go to the Ghetto in Koszalin."

She started to cry.

"There, there," her mother hugged her close. "You'll be O.K. here with us!"

"I know," she whimpered.

"Persecution of our people has become increasingly furious;" Joseph said. "they're now sending hundreds of us to Auschwitch by train every other day."

"That's terrible," Rachel replied.

"Yes, but we're also sending our people out of here so they'll never get on that train. We have an escape plan in effect."

"You do?" Rachel came alive, as though suddenly cured of her brief depression.

"And you know what? We're going to get you out of here tonight. We don't have a moment to lose!"

"Tonight?" Rachel could not believe what she was hearing.

"But Pappa," she quickly continued, "I have just endured a scary home invasion by the Nazis while asleep, hustled into a bus accompanied by guards, with barely anything but the clothes on my back, driven several bumpy hours all the way to Koszalin, then unloaded into the Ghetto. I'm now finally safe in the arms of my beloved parents, who within five minutes want to send me back out again! Talk about roller-coaster emotions!"

"Rachel! Rachel!" Her father began, "We're all being sent to a death camp. It's only a matter of a short time, and we'll all be gone for ever! But fortunately we found out about that, and we've been able to make an escape plan. Like I said, there's no time to waste. You'll not be safe here. We must get you out of here tonight. There's a boat waiting to take you and a few others to Denmark, and from there to Sweden to safety. I'll fill you in on the particulars while we eat. You must get something to eat while you still can. You must be on the bus to Darlawoo at five o'clock. It leaves in less than half an hour! You must hurry!"

"Yes, but how do I get out of the Ghetto now?"

"I'll give you a pass to get out."

"And I just got here!" Rachel lamented. She still had not comprehended the urgency of the situation.

"I know, but you're not safe here. I'm safe here, because of my work as a doctor. I'm needed by everyone, but you'll be sent away as soon as they know you're here, perhaps as soon as tomorrow!"

"Good Grief! I had no idea of all this."

Rachel barely made it to the bus stop at five o'clock and boarded together with five other refugees. They all made it to Darlowoo by nightfall and approached the castle from various directions after dark.

"Hi there, I'm Mark. I'll take you up to the castle and the boat to Denmark. Let me see your passes...OK, just follow me. Please don't run, but move quickly so you don't fall behind!"

They all reached the castle by moving behind the tall bushes along the road.

The guard had just made his turn away from them and headed away from his gate, out toward the far corner of the castle, when Mark made his move for the gate. He waved everyone on, and they followed quickly and silently. This was all so new and sudden for Rachel, and her mind was only half there. She trailed the group just a little, and Mark waved at her to hurry up. She started to run a little, but her right foot stepped on a small rock and twisted inward, causing her to fall to the ground. She got up immediately, but was limping badly from a lot of pain in her ankle. Now far behind the others, she hobbled on.

The guard was nearing the end of his path, and Rachel, getting close to the gate, was still a few yards away. Just as she reached the gate, the guard made his turn.

He couldn't believe what he saw.

A person was actually going through his private gate!

A woman at that.

A woman with a limp.

What was going on?

How could that be?

He had not seen anyone approach the castle before he turned away from the gate.

"Halt! Wer gehest da?" (Stop! Who goes there?)

Mark yanked Rachel inside the gate and steadied her as they both darted quickly through the castle door.

The guard ran down the path.

Thump, thump; thump, thump.

Closer and closer.

Mark and the refugees ran quickly down the long passage to the big hall. Someone else was now helping Rachel, as Mark was out in front of the group. He started to turn the stone in the wall to open the passage to the lower hall and waiting fishing boat.

Rachel was hobbling as fast as she could and came all the way to the hole in the wall when Mark reached out and pulled her through.

They were now both out of sight of the guard.

But they knew he had seen them.

Could they close the opening in time?

As Mark started to turn the stone to close the opening, the guard was right there!

His rifle was pointed directly at Mark.

Mark froze, his hands still on the stone.

No words were spoken.

None were necessary.

The guard entered the passage way, as Mark slowly backed off from the stone.

He had no time to turn the stone and shut the guard out. He had no choice but to retreat.

Rachel had managed to hobble down the stairs out of sight in the darkness. The guard pointed his flashlight at Mark and motioned for him to move down the stairs.

Soon they were all gathered in the lower hall.

They even had a guard. Unfortunately, it was a Nazi guard!

No one said a word as the guard curiously looked around, careful not to lose sight of the rapidly growing group of people, now a total of eight; six refugees, Mark and a fisherman on the boat.

Good grief!

This whole thing was so unexpected, his mind was going a mile a minute.

A boat in here, in a room?

What was all that about?

The guard was bewildered.

He chased everyone aboard the fishing boat, so as to put them all in a small and confined space, easier for him to control.

Or so he thought.

Seeing what was about to happen, Captain Jay managed to duck behind the pilot house before the guard had a chance to spot him.

The guard came aboard and assumed he had everyone in front of him.

"Sie sind alle verhaftet!" (You're all under arrest!)

Still stunned by the circumstances, he paused for another moment. to collect his thoughts.

Here was the great hall he had heard so much about, but never seen.

A secret passage out of the great hall.

A secret lower hall.

A mini harbor inside the castle.

A fishing boat sitting right there, inside the castle!

Who would've thought?

Then a group of people on their way to that boat.

A group of people that had completely escaped his watchful eye in front of the castle.

It was all too much for the poor man to process in his mind all at once.

He was clearly overwhelmed and hesitated to give any further commands.

He needed time to think.

He didn't get much time.

No one said a word.

No one moved a muscle.

They all sensed something was about to happen.

Their hearts pounded in their throats.

Any minute now!

Captain Jay realized that all would be lost if the guard was left alive to tell about it.

It's either him or us!

Jay was like a panther eyeing his prey.

Waiting for that brief and precious moment.

Perhaps the only moment ever.

Jay seized on the guard's moment of hesitation.

A moment in which his intensely overworked brain, occupied by all the new revelations, could not keep up with the rapid pace of unfolding events.

His brain was essentially paralyzed.

He could not respond effectively.

He was lost, if for only a moment.

But that's all it took for Jay to quickly reach for a boat hook next to him behind the pilot house. Seemingly out of nowhere a spear swished through the air, the tip piercing the exposed throat of the guard. He let out a gurgle, as he fell to the deck without another sound.

Mark grabbed the guard's rifle and threw it overboard, as it would be a serious liability if found by a boarding patrol. Jay and Mark struggled to lift the dead guard up over the railing in order to throw him overboard.

"Wait a minute , Mark, I have a better idea."

He held the guard against the railing and said, "It'll not do to have him found here in the river. We'd better dispose of him out at sea."

They secured him to the railing and got ready to cast off. Mark went back up to turn the stone and close the secret entrance. He carefully inspected the halls and stairway for any evidence that anyone had been there. He then jumped aboard, knowing that the passage and lower hall would remain secret. Returning to the boat, he found Jay already at the wheel ready to shove off.

"Jay, hold on a minute," he said. "Before we shove off, I gotta tell you I am concerned about Rachel. She sprained her ankle and can hardly walk. Will it not be too risky to take her along? Look at the problem she caused by being too slow up in front of the castle. She could get you all in trouble at some point. There's still time for me to take her back home to recover"

"What you say could be true, Mark. But this is not a perfect world. We'll face obstacles on our way, we may be saddled with handicaps, but we can't turn back; we can't give up because of all that we have to deal with, expected or unexpected. She must escape just like the rest of them. We can't send her back. We can't send anyone back like unwanted merchandise. We can't send anyone back to a certain death! If she or anyone else gets us into some kind of trouble, we'll deal with it. I did so a moment ago. And I'll do so again. We'll succeed! She may be a handicap to the group crossing Bornholm, but you know what? The Danes are as good if not even better than I am at making things work out. The Danes will get her to Sweden, even if they have to carry her all the way! Ok Mark?"

"Well... OK...Yeah. I admire your courage under fire. You truly are going to make this mission a success."

"Let's shove off!"

Mark cast the stern line off. Jay put the engine in gear and slowly left the dock. Mark chose once more to jump off at the end of the pier at the mouth of the river. Soon Jay was several miles out to sea, and the body of the guard was allowed to slip into the black waters of the Baltic. The body sank quickly with all the heavy gear attached. The refugees had been well hidden as usual.

Jay didn't have to deal with any boarding patrols and arrived at Boderne on Bornholm just as dawn was breaking. The refugees landed safely and were greeted by Hans, as they disappeared into the bushes above the beach. They found a soft place to rest, as they lay down on the sand dunes. Hans sat down next to Rachel.

"Rachel, Captain Jay mentioned that you hurt your ankle last night. How're you doing with that?"

"It hurts a lot, and it's swollen. I can hardly step on it. It sends shocks of pain up the side of my leg."

"Sounds like you can hardly walk."

"I can for a short distance; then I have to stop and rest."

"In that case, you shouldn't walk on it. We're going to cross the island on bicycles, and that'll not be so bad on your ankle. You may have some discomfort, but it'll be a lot better than walking. I hope you'll be OK with that."

"I'll sure try," Rachel replied.

"Great!"

Hans turned to the group.

"Here's our goal for today. We'll rest here till sunrise; then we'll make our way across the island and get to the little town of Tejn on the North Coast by nightfall. Follow me and stay close behind me."

Several hours later, the group set out on the dirt road leading to the highway. Rachel did pretty well initially, then began to fall behind just a little. The group quickly crossed the highway and continued up the road going north toward the center of Bornholm. Rachel crossed the highway just as a Nazi patrol car came over a hill on the western horizon. Rachel didn't notice the car, but the Nazis spotted her as she turned off the road.

The group was now a quarter of a mile ahead of Rachel and way out of sight around a curve in the road. Rachel was pedaling as fast as she could. Her heart leaped into her throat, when she heard the Nazi patrol car turn onto the road behind her.

She broke out in a cold sweat.

She knew the Nazis only too well.

She knew she couldn't outrun the patrol.

Her leg was exhausted from pedaling so fast.

She had to do something.

She had to act quickly.

She turned west off the road.

She found herself in a forest.

The soft ground and many leaves and twigs slowed her down.

She saw the patrol stop out on the road behind her.

There was no doubt they were after her.

She knew what that was like.

She threw the bike down and started to run.

She knew running away was like an admission of guilt.

Guilty of doing something wrong.

Guilty until proven innocent!

A sort of reverse human rights.

She wasn't going to argue with the Nazis.

She ran toward what she knew would be North.

The Nazis had entered the forest.

They had smelled blood.

They were still coming her way.

She could hear their heavy boot steps.

Squish, squish, squish in the leaves and soft ground.

They were getting closer.

She saw a group of old fallen trees behind some bushes.

She quickly threw herself under an old 2 foot thick tree and pulled a smaller one over her as much as possible.

She tried to hold her breath, but she was panting too hard .

She just had to breathe.

She heard the crunching and swishing of the Nazi boots getting very close.

She could hear them whisper.

They wondered where on earth she could have gone.

Please don't find me, was her only thought.

Please don't find me, she kept repeating to herself, like a command the Nazis should obey.

Please don't find me!

Perhaps the good fairy was listening and would be good enough to intervene.

Maybe she was sitting right there on another log, just waiting to hear her wish in order to act on it.

The crunching slowed down.

It stopped a few feet away.

Now she had to hold her breath.

"Ist nieman hier!" (There's no one here)

"Gehe nach links!" (Go to the left)

The Nazis started to run off to the left, going west, as they'd lost her trail and resumed their chase in the previous westerly direction.

Rachel allowed herself to gasp for air till she had made up for holding her breath so long.

She decided to stay right where she was for a while.

She wasn't going to risk running into the Nazis.

They'd probably return to try to pick up her trail again.

With the Nazis out of her immediate vicinity, she began to think about what to do next.

She wondered, had Hans not noticed her absence?

Surely he'd have noticed by now.

She knew he'd come back and look for her.

She just knew he would.

But would he find her before the Nazis came back?

She swept some more leaves over her body to camouflage herself better.

Her leg was pounding.

Her leg really needed a rest.

This was as good a place as any.

The rest would do her good.

She dozed off, exhausted by lack of sleep and the intense physical exertion of the past hour.

A little after passing the first curve in the road, Hans slowed down to drop back and check on Rachel.

"Where's Rachel?" He asked alarmed, as she was nowhere in sight.

The group came to a stop.

"What happened to the car I heard," one of them asked.

"I don't think it passed us," another said.

"I believe it must have stopped behind the curve we just went by," Hans answered, pointing to where they had been.

"We'd better move on quickly. I know a place where you'll be safe, while I return to look for Rachel."

"But shouldn't we all look for her now?"

"And all get shot? I don't think so," Hans replied.

"We can't risk the lives of the entire group to save one!" he continued.

No one said a word as they chewed on that philosophy.

"I know it's difficult to readily accept that concept. I try to explain it to every group I see, but not everybody understands the wisdom that supports it."

"Could you try to explain it to us?"

"OK, it's basically very simple in that many lives are more important than one. However nothing is either pure black or pure white! Everything is relative."

"How's that?"

"Well, sometimes one life may be very crucial to a cause, and the risks to the group, or the many, may be low; and a decision could go the other way. It'll always be a matter of judgment in each case; however the leader must always be aware of the main principle.

71

Try thinking of various scenarios, and you'll see both how simple it is and also how difficult it frequently can be. I hope that helps a little, unfortunately we don't have enough time today for a lengthy discussion of all the pros and cons of that principle."

Soon they reached the church and farm in Åkirkeby, where Hans knew the owner. They all biked right in through the open gate into the courtyard, where the owner came out from the barn this time.

"You've come back Hans. I hope this isn't the same group as last time," he said jokingly.

"No, no, this is quite a new group. They need to hide in a safe place, while I go back and look for one that got left behind." Hans laid it all on the line.

"Oh no, how'd that happen?"

"She has an injured ankle and must've stopped as we rounded a curve.

There may be a Nazi patrol car in the area, so I'd better hurry back. You guys are all safe here."

A second later Hans was turning out of the gate, headed up the road on his bike.

As he rounded the curve that had obscured Rachel, he saw the Nazi patrol car parked on the wrong side of the road, and he knew something was up.

He turned off the road into the forest heading west and hid the bike under a bush. He surveyed the area carefully.

There was no one there.

He heard only a few sparrows and a crow.

A light breeze rustled the leaves of the many oak and birch trees, as he carefully made his way west through the forest.

He angled his path slightly southward to connect with the probable path that Rachel and the pursuing Nazis had taken. He was careful not to step on any branches and cause a loud cracking sound, nor holes in the ground, that might cause him to twist his ankle, or even break a leg.

He slowed down as he passed a cluster of big fallen trees. Someone could be hiding behind them.

They could jump out and surprise him.

He listened for any sound of human movement, like breathing, talking, foot steps, and also sudden noises from a surprised bird or rabbit.

Nothing moved.

He advanced to the other side of the fallen trees.

He just knew someone was hiding in there.

"Hans?" A woman's voice cried out softly.

"Rachel!" He almost shouted. He turned around and saw her well camouflaged with leaves and virtually hidden under the fallen trees.

"Am I glad to see you!" she whispered.

"Me too," he said. "Let's get you out of there."

"Is it safe?"

"Yes, I don't see or hear anyone."

"OK, but two Nazis went by a little while ago, and they might be on their way back by now."

"You're right. You have good common sense," Hans remarked. "We've got to be very careful."

"How's your ankle?" He said as he extracted her from her safe hiding place under the leaves.

"Sore, but I can stand on it a little."

"Can you walk on it a little?"

"I'll try."

"Here, hold on to my arm; we'll work our way back to the road."

They started to walk north together to avoid the direct path back to the patrol car. It was slow going, as Rachel still had a bad ankle.

"Here's a clearing; let's rest a minute," Hans suggested.

"Great!" She said, as she plopped to the ground in the soft high grass on the small meadow. A few birds took flight immediately, as their privacy had been disturbed. Their loud and rapid flapping of the wings expressed their indignation, but might also alert predators, animal or human. A few seconds later a beautiful silence came over the meadow, a typical peaceful Danish forest scene.

"I knew you would be back for me!" Rachel whispered.

"I'm really sorry I didn't see you fall behind like that. I really feel bad about that." Hans admitted.

"Don't be sorry. You too might have been seen by the Nazis, if you had come back right away."

"Maybe so. Let's hope they find their way back to the car and go back where they came from."

"Right!"

"Hände hoch!"

Came a sudden command from behind.

Hans and Rachel jumped to their feet and turned, raising their hands.

The Nazis had gone a little North of their path when returning and had now run right into Hans and Rachel.

The Nazis stomped out into the tall grass on the Meadow to get the sun behind them. They were pointing their pistols at their new prisoners.

Just then a black streak flew by just above the grass, and one of the Nazis jumped a mile, letting out a yell of pain.

"Was ist los?" (What is wrong?) The other asked, perplexed.

The first one had now fallen to the ground, holding his leg with both hands in obvious agony.

A large black viper had let him know that his heavy boots had disturbed its privacy. Two long poisonous fangs had delivered the message at just the right time and place, above the boot, just below the knee.

As the other Nazi quickly checked the bite and put a tourniquet on the leg, Hans and Rachel slowly backed away into the edge of the forest and vanished through the trees. The Nazis were too occupied with their new emergency to notice that they were now alone with one of Denmark's most vicious defenders!

The Nazis were very uneasy, as the tall grass made it impossible to see the viper and from which direction it might return and strike again. The other Nazi did not want to get bit, but he was obligated to help his partner get back to their car. It was a very slow process. By the time they reached their car, Hans and Rachel were long gone.

"How come the high boots didn't protect that soldier?" Rachel asked.

"You want the short or the long answer?"

"Both!"

"OK, the short answer is that he was simply in the wrong place at the wrong time. But seriously, and the long answer is that the viper seeks to strike an area that emits heat. Thus the tall grass forced the viper to lunge higher off the ground, and the area of the knee not covered by the boot emitted a higher temperature.

The large six foot viper, an unusually large specimen, is Denmark's only poisonous snake. Its strike is lighting fast, and its bite can be deadly. It can be compared to the American Rattlesnake, in that most bites cause severe pain and local tissue damage. But if the fangs enter a blood-vessel, and the poison gets widely distributed, the effects can quickly be lethal.

The viper will retreat a little while, letting the poison kill its victim. Shortly thereafter the viper returns, guided by the scent produced by its poison and damaged tissues. It easily finds its victim."

"That's horrible!"

Hans placed Rachel sideways on the cross bar of his bicycle.

"This is the safest place for you to ride. It'll also make it easier for you, as you don't have to pedal the bike."

They soon reached the farm, where the others were waiting, and entered the courtyard to quiet cheers from the group.

"You found her!"

"Are you all right?"

Everyone crowded around for a personal inspection.

"She's fine," Hans assured them, "As long as she sits on my crossbar!"

"Oh, so that's it!"

"What else could I do?" Rachel replied, "my ankle's still pretty bad. And we had a close call with a Nazi patrol, but Hans rescued me. He's my hero! The Nazis surprised us, but a Danish viper took them out of commission right there!"

"Wow, what excitement!"

"Yeah, I think we've had our share for today," Hans continued. "Let's move on."

"Is Rachel going to ride with you again?" someone asked.

"Absolutely," Hans answered.

"Aw, how sweet!"

"Hans, my hero." Rachel said as she jumped up on the cross bar.

At the center of the island, the group now entered the third largest forest in Denmark.

"I wish we could do some sightseeing," Hans said, "but I'm afraid that'll have to wait till you all come back after the war is over."

"You will come back after the war, won't you?" Hans spoke

softly to Rachel, who was able to turn her head toward Hans and look him in the eye.

"Come back after the war? Are you kidding? I don't want to leave!" Rachel said affirmatively as her eyes met Hans's.

He was speechless for a moment, then answered.

"But you must go to Sweden tonight!"

"What if I can't?" Was the coy reply.

"Why not?"

"I can't with this ankle!"

"We'll carry you aboard the boat, and you wouldn't have to take a single step more here in Denmark. Then you can rest your leg all you want in Sweden."

Captain Jay was right. The resourceful Danes would not let anything interfere with their goal of getting all refugees safely to Sweden.

"What if I don't want to?"

"Don't want to what?"

"Go to Sweden!"

"Oh, come on now, you've come this far, have gone through so much, and now you're almost there. Why would you suddenly not want to go all the way?"

"I know I've been through a lot in the past 24 hours, much more than I could possibly have imagined, and much more than I ever want to go through again."

"Well then?"

"But I've also found something I thought I'd never find!"

"What's that?"

Rachel turned and looked at Hans with her large piercing dark eyes. She was silent for a moment, while contemplating the words from the last minutes of conversation and absorbing Hans's perplexed expression.

Does he not feel anything, she thought, he's just got to feel something. He saved my life.

She couldn't reveal her true thoughts right then; she just wasn't ready to put her emotions on her sleeve. But what could she say that would still be convincing enough to satisfy Hans that she really had to stay on Bornholm for now?

"I…I don't know quite how to say this…"

"That's OK, just try. You can tell me."

"It's too personal."

"I won't tell a soul."

Hans took his eyes off the road for a second and looked up. His eyes met Rachel's. A strange sensation came over him. He had never felt this way before. That searching stare of the dark Gypsy like eyes of this beautiful young woman, sitting no more than six inches in front of him, was somehow overwhelming. He was at a loss for words.

His mind seemed to be on hold, as he tried to comprehend what was taking place.

"You promise?" Rachel whispered without taking her eyes off his.

"I promise!"

Rachel had so much pent up emotion. The events of the past 24 hours swirled around in her mind. At one moment she was confused, the next frightened, then relieved, at last immensely grateful. Then she felt something different. Something tingled through her body. It was strange. It was truly weird. It was about to explode! She couldn't contain it. She had to let it out.

"Hans," she finally continued. "You're my hero. You know that don't you?"

"Oh, I suppose so." Hans replied modestly.

"Yes you are. You saved my life back there. You're definitely my hero!"

"OK."

"But you know what?"

"What?"

"You're more than that to me. You're more than just my hero."

"What do you mean?"

"You're someone I've been looking for, for a long, long time."

"Me?"

"Yes, you're not only my hero. You're a hero to a lot of people; but more than that, you're a wonderful, caring person. You always know what to do, and you're always happy. I just can't help but love all that in a man."

"I didn't realize I was all that."

"Hans, I don't want to go to Sweden because I want to be with you! Can you understand that?"

"I think so, and I would really love to have you stay on Bornholm, but you would not be safe here; and what's more, I'm obligated to get you safely to Sweden," Hans answered, returning to reality.

"I know, but don't I have anything to say about it? It's my life isn't it? Am I not allowed to decide my own fate?"

"Well, I suppose you are, but what would your parents say?"

"About what?"

"About you not going to Sweden."

"They'd be shocked and concerned for my safety."

"That's right."

"But I know they'd understand if I told them I had found a very special person and chose to be with him."

Hans began to realize that the woman sitting six inches in front of him was actually serious about him.

His mind reeled from the unexpected surge of emotion. He tried to make sense of it all, causing a traffic jam of thoughts. It was as if his saving her from the clutches of the Nazis had made her feel that now he owned her; she now belonged to him. He had saved her, so now she was his.

Forever!

Oh boy! What had he gotten himself into now?

But those big dark eyes had stared into his and pierced them, with an expectant stare that also pierced his soul. It had penetrated so deep it gave him sensations he had never had before. That stare had ignited a spark; that spark of chemistry known to be able to change lives forever. He knew. This was one special woman.

The sun was setting, and the group was closing in on Tejn. Hans picked a small farm road lined by tall bushes to stop and rest to wait for darkness, before entering the small village of Tejn. Hans took Rachel aside and tried to come to some agreement about her plans.

"You know Rachel," he began, "your bad ankle will not do as a reason for you to stay here on Bornholm. As I mentioned before, you'll not need to walk even five steps before you'll be in Sweden!"

"I realize that now. You've really been able to solve any and all problems with our passage across Bornholm, and that's very impressive, but just the same, I really do want to stay here."

"If you're intent on staying here, how'll you then explain that to the rest of your group?"

"Well, first of all, they're not really 'my' group. I don't share anything with them other than escaping together.

And second of all, you're the one that's helped me. I don't owe them an explanation or anything else."

"That's true, but you know they'll be shocked, and they'll ask why you would reject safety for something else."

"Yes, but I can deal with that. I have my personal reasons, and only you and I know what they are."

"OK then, but you'll have to stay somewhere, and maybe you'll want to go to Sweden at a later date. You know you can always do that. Any time you wish, just say the word, and you'll be on the boat!"

"That's good to know, and thank you so very much for that, but I don't think that'll come up for a while. Do you know any families here in Tejn, or elsewhere for that matter, that could use a maid, a cook, or other help in their business in return for room and board?"

Her plans were getting deeper and deeper. Hans had not anticipated that sort of thing. Who'd have thought a refugee would deviate from the express route to freedom and safety? And then already think of long term arrangements? There was a lot more to this girl than meets the eye, he thought.

"As a matter of fact, I do know a family here in Tejn that needs some help in their business."

"What kind of business?"

"It's a Smoked Herring plant."

"What could I do there?"

"They get the fresh Herring from the fishermen; then they hang them up on long wires above a large fireplace where they are smoked till they are a golden brown color. Then they're taken down and packed in containers. Some are sold right here, but most are shipped to restaurants in Rønne or Copenhagen. The job is really easy, and you might just get to eat a few fish!"

"How do you know all that?"

"I grew up here, so I know it personally."

"Do you know the family well?"

"Yes, it's my girlfriend's family."

"Your girlfriend?"

"Yes."

"Does she live there too?"

"Yes."

Rachel took a deep breath. Now it was her mind that was racing.

I hadn't expected Hans to have a girlfriend, with his dangerous escapades and traveling all over. Oh well, that doesn't change how I feel about him. And why wouldn't he have a girlfriend, a wonderful guy like him?

It would be strange if he didn't have one or more girls in love with him. Actually, that might even prove to be an advantage! I'll be certain to see more of him, as he'd undoubtedly visit that house more than any other.

And if I can just prove myself better than the competition, then all's going to be fine, just fine.

You know what? I'm going to go for it!

No other option is going to work, because if I stay somewhere else, I might never see Hans.

Yes, this is going to be OK.

And wait, I suddenly have a great idea, but I'll keep it a secret for now. It'll keep until my ankle gets better; then it'll be a perfect means to winning the man of my dreams.

"You know what, Hans?" She continued. "I really don't mind. I'd love to help out in a small business like that."

"Are you sure?"

"Yes, I'm sure."

"I mean staying at my girlfriend's house?"

"Yes, as long as there's room for me."

"OK then, we'll go there after the boat leaves."

"Oh, thank you, thank you," Rachel threw her arms around the embarrassed Hans and kissed him on the cheek. He turned a bright pink, as he suddenly saw the group watching them.

"What was all that about?" one of them asked.

"Hans just found a job for me!" Rachel said quickly.

"You don't say! Can he find one for us too?"

"I don't think you'll want one like that," Hans replied.

"Why not?"

"It's right here in Tejn, here on Bornholm."

"No thanks, we need one in Sweden."

"I thought so. The Swedes'll help you there."

Hans delivered the group to Nils's fishing boat after parking the bikes in a small shed by a fisherman's house.

When all had come aboard except Rachel, Nils asked,

"Is she not part of the group? Is she not coming with us?"

"No, she's going to stay and work here in Tejn." Hans informed.

"You're joking, aren't you?"

"No, I'm serious."

"You don't think I can work here in Tejn?" Rachel asked indignantly.

"Oh, I don't doubt you can, but it could be dangerous. You'd better keep her well hidden, Hans."

"She'll be fine. You'd better get out of here."

"See you later." Nils jumped aboard and was soon out of sight in the darkness of the night.

"Come, let's go find your new boss and new home."

Rachel jumped up on the cross bar again, and Hans headed for a small pink house with a green turf roof two hundred feet from the edge of the water. He knocked softly on the door of the darkened house. The door opened revealing a blinding light inside a cozy living room. The two entered quickly, closing the door behind them. The house was again invisible in the darkness.

"This is Rachel," Hans began. "She's come from Poland this morning and would like very much to stay here and work, rather than go to Sweden. How do you like that?"

Ole Petersen was a burly man in his mid fifties, having smoked Herrings out in back of his house in his little "factory" all his life.

"Welcome to Bornholm, Rachel," he reached for her hand. "I could use an assistant right here." He looked searchingly at Rachel, as if she might possibly be one.

"I thought you might," Hans said. "Would that be OK with you?" He looked at Rachel.

"Just fine! I'd love to. Thank you so much!"

"Then it's settled," Ole said quickly before anyone could have time to change their mind. "You can start in the morning."

"I'd like nothing better, but I hurt my ankle pretty bad last night, and I can hardly stand on it. I really need a day or two of rest to recover." Rachel said, immediately taking control of her own affairs.

"That's OK. Just let me know when you are ready," Ole said. He was a down to earth straight-shooter, taking life as it came, minute by minute.

"One other thing," Hans continued. "Rachel will need a place to live. She's willing to trade room and board for work. Can you handle that too, Ole?"

"Oh, you want to live right here with us? Yeah, we have a small spare room you could have. Yeah... that'll be OK."

"Wonderful, then it's all settled." Rachel said with a deep sigh. "Thank you so very much Mr. Petersen."

"Just call me Ole."

"OK, Ole, I'll do that."

"Come, I'll show you to your room."

Ole and Hans helped Rachel get situated; then everyone went their separate ways.

CHAPTER 11

The sun peeked over the horizon. The long red and gold beams of light cast a peaceful spell on the sleepy little village of Tejn. The fishermen were still asleep. They had come in during the very early morning, leaving their catch in Ole's smoke factory for him to process. If it weren't for a few early birds already chirping away in the trees, there would be no sign of life.

Ole was up at the crack of dawn. He went out and weighed the trays of Herring stacked up in his little smoker on the side of the house. The total for the night was close to 1000 lbs., a decent night's catch. Content that his work was waiting for him as usual, he woke the rest of the family up for breakfast

"Set an extra place at the table, would you please. We're having a newcomer stay with us for a while." Ole announced. "Her name is Rachel, and she'll be helping me with the fish. She'll be staying in the spare room, and, ...oh, here she comes now. This is Rachel, and this is my wife and our daughter Ulla."

"Hi Rachel, where did you come from?"

"What are you doing in Tejn?"

"How long are you staying?"

Rachel was amused at their intense curiosity, but then newcomers were pretty rare in these parts.

She was hesitant to reveal her origin and intentions to people she didn't know yet, but if she shouldn't say anything to these people, Hans would've told her.

But she'd better make sure for herself, just in case.

"I know all of you are good friends of Hans, right?"

"Oh, yes, that we are," they all chimed in.

"And you know the things Hans is doing, right?"

"There isn't a thing we don't know about Hans!"

"Even helping…eh?"

"You mean helping refugees to cross the island?"

"Yes, yes. Then it's all right that I tell you I was one of them!" Rachel said, relieved of the burden of secrecy.

"I escaped from the Nazis in Poland and came across the island with the group that went on to Sweden last night."

"Really? Then why aren't you also on your way to Sweden?" Ulla asked pointedly.

"I chose to stay in Denmark, partly because I hurt my ankle very bad last night, and I can hardly stand on it yet. I really need to rest and recover."

"Then you'll be going on to Sweden next week, I presume?" Ulla continued.

"No, I've decided to stay here in your lovely little town and work with Ole, eh…Mr. Petersen, here as his assistant in return for staying in your back room."

"In that case welcome to our home," Mrs. Petersen said.

"Well, you'll find Tejn to be a very small town," Ulla said dryly.

"Too small for another young girl?"

"Perhaps," Ulla replied cleverly, "but you'll find out for yourself as you get to know everybody. We're like one big family, but we do have as many as 270 people here in Tejn."

"I just love your town, and I know I'll get to love your people too." Rachel said.

"That's what I'm afraid of," Ulla whispered to her mother.

Ole felt a bit of rising tension between the two young women and didn't want to be caught in the middle of it. He decided to defuse it before it had time to gather more steam.

"I'm very happy to finally have some help with the work," he said hurriedly, "but Rachel will need to recover for a couple of days before she can help me. So don't you ask her to help until then. Well, the fish are waiting for me. I hear them! I hear them!" He chanted as he got up and left the room.

"Come and sit down," Ulla invited.

"Have you known Hans very long?" Rachel asked.

"Quite a while! We were both born right here."

"Wow, you've lived here all your lives?"

"Yes, so we know each other very well." Ulla said smiling, knowing she had scored one for herself, able to lay claim to Hans by having known him first, and that for an incontestably long time.

Ulla had grown up with Hans. No one could have known each other better than they did.

And yet, they were still just friends.

They were not engaged and obviously had not wished to move toward marriage.

To Rachel that meant an opportunity for her to enter the scene as a fresh new face and body and to break the apparent stalemate, so to speak. She thought the chance of her being able to sweep Hans away from the competition was quite good; in fact, it looked exceptionally good.

Rachel was not discouraged in the least; she was a born optimist. To her a glass was never half empty; it was always half full. Rachel also knew she had a secret weapon, soon to be deployed; one that would clinch the success of any battle over Hans. But for now, she held her tongue.

"That's really great," she said.

Her answer had a double meaning.

One for Ulla.

One for Rachel.

It was a perfectly balanced reply.

It had poured oil on stormy waters.

Peace was restored, for the moment.

CHAPTER 12

Three days later Rachel was back on her feet and working happily with preparing a thousand Herrings for placement in the smoker. They were gathered on a thick wire that was hung in slots on both sides of the smoking chamber, an open area between the burning wood and the 12 foot cone shaped chimney. It was a far cry from her old job as a librarian in Poland; but, hey, she was game to try anything new, especially if she could be with the man of her dreams.

"Hey Rachel, how're you doing?" a familiar voice rang through the alley between the house and the smoker.

"Hans! I'm so glad to see you. I thought you might've forgotten all about me." Rachel exclaimed as she threw her arms around his neck and kissed him on the cheek.

Hans looked into her eyes and was again mesmerized by that captivating look of the two dark eyes of this vivacious woman.

"I could never forget all about you!" He said. "I'm afraid you've made a lasting impression on me."

"Don't be afraid, I come in peace!" She said with a smile.

"Oh, I'm not afraid. And by the way, you have a great smile; but you didn't show me that the other day, you know."

"I wasn't quite myself that day."

"You look happier today, all right."

"I'm glad you noticed," she said.

"So tell me," Hans asked as he slipped out of her strangle hold on his neck, "how're you getting on here, with the fish and all that?"

"The fish and I have made friends; your girlfriend is something else!"

"How so?"

"I don't think she's too friendly."

"Well, you know, she's not very comfortable with strangers. She's grown up in this really small town."

"She told me that, but so have you, right?"

"Yeah, but I get around a lot more. I'm used to all kinds of people."

"Even someone like me?"

"No, but I've gotten quite used to you already."

"But you've only known me for a few days."

"Yes, but I've learned a lot about you in that short time."

"How did you do all that?"

"By watching you. By listening to you."

"And what've you learned from that?"

"That you are a very courageous and determined young woman."

"Is that all?"

"I think that's already quite a lot!"

"But you've learned more than that, right?"

"Yes, there's a lot more!"

"Tell me, tell me!"

"Not before you tell me some more about yourself."

"OK, what more can I tell you?"

"You said you worked as a librarian at the main library in Szczecin, right?

"Yes."

"What was that like?"

"I enjoyed access to a world of books right at my fingertips. I was able to choose a book to read in between handling customers at the check-out desk, where I also met hundreds of people, young and old, men and women. I could chat with all of them, longer with some than others. Some eligible bachelors interested me, but they were few and far between. None of them made any lasting impression on me.

Then, after a few years, I started to get discouraged."

"Why?"

"I began to wonder if there really was someone out there just waiting to meet me, and if so, where was he? How long did I have to wait before he showed up? Or was all that a myth?"

"Sounds like you were really in the wrong place."

"That's right, and I'm through waiting. Can you understand that? I want to take my life in my own hands for a change. I'm determined to do something to change it. This whole series of events has been the last straw! What if my life suddenly came to an end? Yes, I'm definitely through waiting!"

"Yes, I can understand that."

"Then for some reason I became incredibly lucky. It was as if someone up there had granted my wish. Do you know that at the same instant I decided to take action, the man of my dreams appeared. Can you believe that? It was like magic. But however it's come about, I'm not going to refuse to make the most of it."

"Tell me more."

"I think my long suppressed aggressive side has been awakened by these near fatal experiences, and it's as though I've been reborn. Life is no longer going to pass me by.

I'm going to reach out and grab it.

I'm not afraid of competition.

In fact, I welcome it As I see it, it's the best and most natural way for a woman to establish her own worth, and I'm quite confident of myself as a woman.

I'm already using one of my talents.

My versatility.

A librarian turned fish smoker?

That has to be a first!"

"You're right about that."

And if that wasn't enough, she said to herself, I also have a secret weapon! A very secret weapon, and the time for me to use it is coming fast.

"Now it's your turn to tell me about your thoughts."

"I'd like to, but it'll take a while, and I must go."

"Then tell me tonight, after supper."

"I can't. I have important business to attend to."

"More refugees to guide across the island?"

"No, this is different."

"Can you tell me?"

"It's part of the secret resistance."

"We both hate the Nazis. You know I'm 100% on your side"

"I know. I've got to go to the top of the island this evening and will not return till sometime after midnight."

"Gosh Hans, it sure is hard to get you to open up more. I know you have to be extremely careful not to reveal any secrets to anyone, even to me. But, you know I've been persecuted by the Nazis and would never reveal any secrets."

I think the time has come to use my secret weapon, she thought. I feel I'm ready for action!

"Hans," she began, "I want to join the Danish Resistance!"

"You what?"

"I want to join up and fight against the Nazis. I want to help all I can."

"Do you know how dangerous that is?"

"Of course I do. Haven't I seen that just a few days ago?"

"I guess you have at that."

"Then take me with you tonight! I really want to be part of your group."

"Look Rachel, I can well see that you're determined at all costs to join the efforts to fight the Nazis. And I know you wouldn't hesitate to do whatever it takes to defend yourself and others; but you're still only a civilian, and not a freedom fighter like we are."

"But Hans haven't I proven myself to be quite resourceful in evading the Nazi patrol in spite of my injured ankle. And I've braved the Baltic passage in a Sardine can type of hiding place. That's a lot more than most people can claim to have experienced, don't you think?"

"All right Rachel, you convinced me. Get your hat and coat and let's get going. I'll tell Ole you'll be working with me until after midnight."

"Oh thank you, thank you. You'll never regret it. You don't know how much this means to me."

"You can tell me later."

Hans and Rachel grabbed a couple of bikes and took off toward the northern tip of Bornholm.

"What we're going to do tonight is pick up a load of weapons that'll be dropped by an RAF (British Royal Air Force) bomber. Six of us have arranged to meet at the drop site and take the weapons away immediately, and bring them to safety, and at the same time avoid any run-in with the Nazis."

"I'm going to have to ask you a lot of basic questions. I hope you won't mind?"

"No. Go right ahead."

"How do you know where the drop site is?"

"We listen to the BBC (British Broadcasting Company) every night, and during a special 5 minute segment right after a certain hour, the time and location of the drop is given in a coded message. I can't tell you exactly how right now, but the RAF varies the time and location every week to keep the Nazis off our trail. It won't be long before I can show you where it'll be tonight."

"Does that happen every week?"

"So far it has, but only if we hear the right message; then it's always a few days later."

"Have the Nazis ever found all that out?"

"No, but there've been a couple of times they heard the plane and figured something was about to happen. We saw them searching all over the place, but they never found anything."

"Wow! That's really a daring thing to do, almost right in front of their noses!"

"It's unavoidable if we're to have any weapons and strengthen the resistance groups."

"That's amazing."

"We try very hard to avoid any confrontations with the Nazis. If we ever should have a run-in with them, we'll always retreat immediately to a solid cover, such as rocks, trees, small hills, or mounds, etc. From there we look for a further way back from the area. The reason for that is that we'll nearly always be outgunned and outnumbered by them. They have many soldiers, many machine guns and hand grenades. The absolutely most important thing to remember is to take cover. A cover is your life! You can shoot all you want from behind a cover, but without a cover, you'll be the one that gets shot!"

"How do you manage to get out of the area unseen with the weapons?"

"We approach the drop site from all sides, so that each of us can lead all the others back out from the area by the same way we came in, if needed. That way we also have the area surrounded and can better keep watch for Nazis. We would also have an advantage if the Nazis should invade the site and surprise us; if we were forced to counter attack, they'd not expect us to attack from all sides at once."

"Who picks the drop site locations?"

"We have pre-approved a number of sites. The RAF chooses a different one each week, then sends us the coded message telling us when and where."

"Where do you then take the weapons?"

"Each of us is responsible for several weapons. That way, if anyone should be discovered, it would not affect all the others."

"That sounds smart."

"Well, here we are. We'll go over there and hide the bikes and walk the rest of the way."

Hans and Rachel walked cautiously through a forested area and approached a small meadow from the east, so as to have a clear view of the western sky. Hans continued the briefing in a near whisper.

"The drops are always made very precisely at the designated time in order to minimize our exposure to discovery. We arrive five minutes before drop time and check in with each other, then scatter and wait out of sight at the edge of the clearing. We keep a sharp lookout and listen carefully. Everyone has a flashlight with red and green covers for signaling, but I'm always the first one to signal the plane, unless I become disabled in some way."

The group readily accepted Rachel, when they learned that she'd not been out of Hans's sight since the early afternoon, a vital security consideration for a newcomer. The questions Rachel asked could have aroused suspicion that she might be a German spy, but since she was the persecuted daughter of the designer of the escape plan and had shown such heroic behavior, that suspicion was dropped.

It was one minute to drop time.

The forest was dead quiet.

The sky was pitch black.

The faint drone of a plane could be heard, quickly getting louder.

Hans was facing west, from which the plane was expected.

The site was clear and secure.

The plane was now close.

It was coming in straight from the West.

Hans gave the signal.

A green S.O.S. repeatedly.

The plane was invisible.

It had no lights.

The plane streaked by directly overhead.

The cargo would already have been dropped.

No one moved.

No one wanted to get hit by a sac of weapons.

It was dead quiet again.

The silence was broken by the rapid breaking of branches. Next a loud thud was heard, as a well padded sack hit the soft ground at the edge of the clearing. It landed just a few feet away from Hans.

Special delivery from RAF to Hans.

"Those RAF guys are incredibly accurate; they practically hit my flashlight!" He said, as he reached down and untied the sac. The others converged on the sac, and each picked up two pistols and a machine gun.

Suddenly several light beams lit up the sky. They crisscrossed frantically, illuminating clear air.

No cloud was seen. No plane was seen.

By now it was far away, crossing Denmark on its way safely back to England.

"We have Nazis close by," Hans whispered, "they must've been in the area and heard the plane."

"Yeah, and they were ready with searchlights."

"Except they were too late!"

"Let's get out of here," Hans commanded.

Carrying their weapons, they all headed west toward the cliffs by the sea, only a quarter of a mile away.

The Nazis were closing in from all sides except the sea. They were sure no one could come or go from that direction, because of the steep and dangerous cliffs and crashing waves down below. Hans and his little group quickly reached the edge of the cliffs. From many years of local knowledge, Hans led the group down through a narrow crevice. Foothold was precarious, and the rocks were wet and slippery from ocean spray. No one dared go there, especially at night, except Hans and his group. Once down, they proceeded slowly southward over the slippery rocks, out of sight and reach by the Nazis, left empty handed at the top of the cliffs. Soon they reached the flat sandy beaches north of the small town of Hasle and climbed up over the hills to the coast highway.

Again the Nazis never found a thing.

No plane, no weapons, no people. Nothing!

But they heard the plane.

That was all they got this time.

That's all they ever got.

Hans and Rachel arrived back in Tejn at 2 O'clock in the morning. They hid the weapons in an old wooden chest that had been buried in the sand, with the lid 3-4 inches underground. After closing the lid on several dozen weapons, sand was scraped back over the lid, and no one but the man on the moon was any wiser.

"That's really clever," Rachel exclaimed quietly, "how long has that been there?"

"Most of the year," Hans replied.

"Hans," Rachel whispered, waiting for him to stop and look at her in the dim light from their flashlights, "I'm really very grateful that you let me join up with you. This is so exciting; it sure beats smoking fish!"

"I bet it does! Just remember, it may be fun when it all goes well, and we can put one over on the Nazis. But you don't want to know how it'll be if it doesn't."

"Have you had some that didn't go well?

"No, but we've had some close calls."

"Would you consider tonight a close call?"

"No, we had plenty of time and space. Close calls are when you expect bullets to come your way any moment."

"Or when you're looking at a gun pointed at you by a Nazi."

"Right, that's very close. Too close!"

"Tell me, how is it possible to pull this off so easily time after time?" Rachel asked.

"There're many reasons for that, and many factors that have to be just right for it all to work."

"Like what?"

"First of all, the geography of Bornholm is ideal for this mission. The northwest corner is long and narrow, requiring only a few minutes of flight over land, meaning only a few minutes of risk to the plane.

The RAF plane can come in directly from the West to avoid making a sharp and noisy banking maneuver that would make it easy for the Nazis to localize it. Coming in low from the ocean, it can make the drop right by the shore, the weapons package coasting a quarter of a mile inland to the clearing. The plane then continues with only a slight turn to the North, crossing quickly over the narrow tip of the island at 150 miles an hour, and is way out over the ocean in a flash. The search lights can't spot the fast moving plane at such low altitude."

"All right, what else?"

"The goal then is for us to quickly get into the clearing, secure the weapons and get out. That's why precise timing is crucial.

A slight delay in getting out of the area could have dire consequences. Careful planning has determined the location of soft ground for landing the goods; easy access for both men and plane; several escape routes, one a secret known only to us; perfect timing with respect to darkness (no full moon!) and low tide to provide escape by the sea below the cliffs."

"It really is fascinating how well planned all this is."

"It has to be. The long term success of sabotage and resistance, armed or otherwise, depends completely on the ability to survive and fight another day.

That means meticulous avoidance of confrontations.

It means setting limited goals, such as stealing or destroying weapons or records of planned activities, lists of freedom fighters or equipment, vehicles, and shipment of weapons."

"Hans, don't take this the wrong way," Rachel moved closer to him, "but I seem to get a thrill out of flirting with danger, like tonight. It doesn't mean that I like playing with fire, or that I am overly confident that nothing bad can happen, it's just that the very possibility of danger puts you on your guard a lot more than otherwise; it seems to heighten your awareness of everything, it sharpens your senses. You know what I mean?"

"Yeah, I know exactly what you mean. It's a way of life for us."

The warm embers from the smoker close by cut the chill of the night. The light smoke made it a cozy atmosphere, not unlike the old Danish Christmas tradition of burning pine branches. Hans saw it coming; but he had no intention of moving away.

"Hans, I wish you didn't have to leave again."

She pulled him closer. He put his arms around her and drew her even closer, if that were possible.

"Well, I do have to get some sleep, you know."

Rachel had moved within striking distance and now reached up and stopped the conversation with a passionate kiss.

Minutes went by.

The two came up for air.

No words were necessary.

They separated slowly, their eyes fixed on each others.

Hans broke the silence, as he whispered softly, "I'll be back tomorrow."

CHAPTER 13

Hans slept late. In fact, he barely made it up by noon. He lived in a small yellow house one street away from the sea. He lived there all by himself, ever since his parents had died four years ago. He liked the freedom of being all by himself. He could go wherever he wanted and do whatever he wanted. He didn't have to answer to anyone.

Such independence had become part of him. It made him well suited for his role as the leader of the Danish Resistance on the island. He started as a fisherman in his youth, but soon settled into the craft of boat building and repair. He also repaired fishing nets.

Oh, why can't this work be steady like other people's? He thought. It always comes in waves. Sometimes I've got more work than I can handle; then at other times I've got very little if any. The only good thing about that is that it fits well with my work in the Resistance. Like now, I have this huge job here that's going to take at least a week to do. How am I ever going to do that? Look at that big hole in the net.

A knock on the door interrupted his thoughts.

"Well Hi there Ulla," he said, as he opened the door.

"Hi Hans, I see you're busy today."

"Yeah, well, actually today I'm mainly thinking."

"What about?"

"How to fix this big crazy hole."

"How'd that get there?"

"One of the boats was out in rough weather the other day and his net got caught up in the propeller. I guess a wave carried it around the stern of the boat and refused to let go. It all happened so fast that it got hopelessly entwined around the shaft and had to be cut free, once the boat was pulled up on the beach."

"I wish I had a job where all I had to do was think.

My work as an artist, decorating souvenirs from Tejn and the North Coast with paint is a very intense and exact job, where small brush strokes are applied to very small areas, requiring a steady hand and a good eye. It gets very tiring after a while."

"Don't tell me you can do that kind of work without any thinking," Hans objected.

"No, but I do get tired of the physical part."

"It's gotta be better than chopping wood!"

"Oh Hans, don't be so dramatic!"

"OK, but you don't look any worse for wear."

"Thanks a lot! Now tell me Hans, what's the story on this new girl Rachel?"

"There's not much to it. She's been persecuted by the Nazis, and now she's decided to help us fight them."

"So its true, she's joined the Resistance?"

"Yeah, it didn't take her long to decide."

"You got that right, she just barely got here! Are you sure you can trust her?"

"She hates Nazis."

"OK then, does she know how to do anything?"

"You mean fighting Nazis?"

"Yeah, she's the only woman I've seen wanting to do that."

"I know, but she's quite intense about it. She seems to have a knack for it. She knows how to protect herself and how to avoid the Nazis. I think she'll do fine."

"Who would've thought?"

"Surprised you didn't it!"

"I think we were all surprised to hear it. It just doesn't seem like woman's work."

"Well, that may be true; but some women are real fighters, you know."

"I see she's convinced you of that."

"Time will tell, but so far so good."

"Do you like her?"

Ulla was getting more concerned that Rachel might be more of a threat than first imagined.

"She's all right. She's very friendly."

That's what I was afraid of, Ulla thought.

"How friendly? She asked, starting to get more inquisitive.

"How do you mean?"

"Is she starting to get personal?" Ulla just had to know.

"You know all women want to get personal with me. I can't help that!"

"I knew it. I knew it!"

"What?"

"She's starting to fall for you!"

"Is that what you came over to talk about?" Hans had suspected that from the start.

"Well, yes and no. I haven't seen you in a while, and well, you know, a girl gets curious."

"Oh, come here," Hans said, as he reached out for her and pulled her close. "You're still my best girl, you know."

"Are you sure?"

"I'm sure. Now go back and do some thinking and apply those paints in a pretty fashion!"

Ulla left by the back door.

Hans focused his eyes on a large seagull sitting on a fencepost close to the open backdoor, clearly waiting for a handout. He threw a piece of French bread at the bird. It casually opened its beak, allowing the bread to enter; then closed its beak and sat motionless as if nothing had ever happened.

"I know you are staring at me," he began talking to the bird. "In case you're wondering what I'm thinking about, here're my thoughts. You see, bird, it's like this.

I've had enough of this "women's curiosity". I realize I'm soon going to be torn between two women, if I'm not already in that predicament. I'm not exactly happy about these overt challenges to my emotions. Now, I know I'll be able to sort it all out eventually, but I definitely need to do something now to free my mind for more pressing matters. I definitely need some space here. But how do I get it? These two women are all over me at close quarters. You know what I mean, don't you."

The bird gave a squawk.

"See, I know you do; and you just fly up higher when you need more space. I'd love to be able to do that too. So, here's the problem.

I've known Ulla all my life, and she is a good friend. But I've never before felt the excitement I feel when I'm in the close presence of Rachel. There's something fiery alive in her that Ulla lacks. Or is it just that my personality seems to click with Rachel's?"

The bird squawked again.

"You see, Ulla is more sedate, even keeled, so to speak, typical of many Danes; quite contrary to Southern Europeans and perhaps Jewish women too. I've never known anyone like Rachel."

The bird tilted its head and looked straight at Hans.

"Don't look at me like that! It's true! And that's the problem. I see it now. I've really never known any women well other than Ulla. It's true, I get around a lot more and know many different people, but still, they're mostly Danes, and most of them even tempered like me. Yeah, that's what it is. I'm a typical Dane, and one of the even tempered guys. No wonder Rachel stands out from the crowd. She's electrifying. She's so much more alive than anyone I've ever known. Maybe the sleepy little town of Tejn has put everyone to sleep; but if so, it hasn't taken long for a woman like Rachel to wake us up. She woke me up all right! I can't fall asleep now. I can't fall asleep without thinking about her. She even wakes me up at night! No woman has ever done that to me before, not ever!"

The bird gave a series of squawks and flapped its wings

"Don't laugh, that's really how I feel! But the question is, will she always be like that? Just assume for the moment that I chose her for my permanent woman in life, would she always remain like she is, or would she gradually loose that spark of life that sets her apart from other women. Would that spark be lost when we settled down or with the passage of time? Who could answer those questions? Probably no one. That would be a gamble I'd have to take with my life. Or was that the only approach? Perhaps Rachel herself could provide those answers. I definitely need to explore that as soon as I can."

"Oh, this hole is just too big to repair," he shouted out loud, scaring the bird off the fence post..

"Oh, I'm so sorry! I really didn't mean to scare you. We've become friends. But then, you never really gave me an answer to my problem. I guess I'll have to find it myself. Ah, yes, that's what you had in mind telling me wasn't it. Smart bird! It sure helped talking to you."

"Now look at this hole! But you know what? I've just found the answer to that. It's obvious. I'll have to splice a whole new section of netting to it, or it'll never be able to float properly. It sure was good talking to that bird; he straightened out my thoughts all right.

My thinking finally solved the fishing net problem; now on to the next!

Uh, oh, it's getting late. I have to get to the South Coast to pick up refugees. Time sure flies, not just when you're having fun, but also when you get deeply into thinking about things!

He ran out the door, jumped on his bike and headed for Boderne, anxious to see what Captain Jay would bring this time.

CHAPTER 14

Ulla felt rather uneasy after her visit with Hans. He had tried to assure her that she was still his favorite girlfriend, but what did that mean?

Ulla began thinking so hard she actually talked to herself.

Could she be his favorite and someone else be his superfavorite? Could she be his favorite girlfriend and someone else be his favorite lover? Or am I just letting my imagination run wild? I hate to think like that, but I am beginning to have doubts about my relationship with Hans?

It never really occurred to me that there could ever be someone else in his life. After all, we've grown up together, gone to school together, played together, even worked together now and then. Our families know each other well, as do most families in our small town of Tejn. As the years go by, it seems only natural that Hans and I are a couple.

He's my man, and I'm his woman.

But now, for the first time, the first time in my entire life, I feel unsure of that.

Things just don't seem the same between us.

Suddenly a light went on in her mind, and her thoughts became more focused.

Could it be that Hans was actually falling for that new refugee?

Could he suddenly have become infatuated with her? No, Hans was not a passionate man to the extent that he would fall for a flirtatious woman.

Or was he?

And she just got here! That raised another important question.

Why was she here?

She had chosen to stay in Denmark and fight the Nazis, rather than seek refuge in Sweden.

Was she nuts?

She had to be out of her mind.

But then again, we stay here too don't we, and we're not nuts. Or are we?

We could escape to Sweden any time we want, but we don't.

We stay and fight.

Maybe she's not nuts after all.

Maybe she's actually clever.

That's it!

She's very clever!

She hates the Nazis.

She wants revenge for past humiliation and suffering; her own, her family's, and her people's! The opportunity was presented to her, and she grabbed it.

And then there's Hans.

Perhaps he's the spark that made her blossom into this love struck freedom fighter!

I know she's love struck.

I know she's got her eyes on Hans.

Maybe more than just her eyes!

Yes, that's it!

It all fits together.

Being close to Hans.

Being a freedom fighter in his group.

Working with him and thrashing the Nazis is one big fantasy come true!

What more could she ask for at this time in her life?

I see it all now.

And the worst part of it is that she's younger than I am.

She's prettier than I am.

She's smarter than I am.

She's more aggressive than I am.

Hey, I may have been replaced here!

Hans may really have replaced me with a young, pretty, clever, and aggressive instant female freedom fighter!

How do you like that?

All in the blink of an eye.

All in the flash of a few days!

Ulla's thoughts were running wild, as she sat in the living room and stared out the window at the sea. It was a beautiful view through the scattered low-cut bushes on the top of the sand. The low clouds made the sea look gray and dreary, a perfect match for her depressed mood.

"Hi Ulla!" The door opened, and her parents entered. "Are you ready for afternoon coffee?"

"Am I ever!" She answered. "I need to talk with you about something."

"Oh, oh. That sounds serious!" Ole said.

"Yeah, you hardly ever seem to have the need to talk about anything serious," her mother chided.

"Here, let's sit down and have some coffee and Danish pastry."

"Ah, that hot coffee sure hits the spot," Ole said, but let's hear what's on your mind Ulla"

"Maybe it's just me, but I'm concerned about Hans," Ulla continued.

"How so?" Her mother asked.

"Well, you know we've been close friends for many years, and I thought we'd get married some day, maybe after the war."

"Go on."

"I have a feeling that things may be changing between us."

"How's that?"

"I think Hans is falling for Rachel," Ulla volunteered softly.

"You don't say!" Her mother exclaimed.

"I'm not surprised," Ole intervened.

"You're not surprised?" Ulla retorted, "what do you mean by that?"

"To answer that, you need to take a good look at your life-long relationship with Hans. It's true it's been a life long friendship, and that's exactly what it is, nothing more, nothing less."

"How can you say that?" Ulla asked tearfully.

"I have seen you and Hans together. I have seen you grow up together for quite a few years. And I've seen you as grown-ups for quite a few years as well."

"We've known each other all our lives."

"Twenty six years to be exact; and that's exactly the point!"

"What's exactly the point?"

"After all this time, are you not still just friends?"

"No, we're more than just friends."

"You may think so, but a relationship between a man and a woman needs to move forward with time; it has to get somewhere. It might not go forward quickly. It may have pauses on the way, and even though it may move forward slowly, it must move forward."

"Or what?"

"It fades. It must be nourished and allowed to grow as a result. Your relationship with Hans has gone nowhere for years and years."

"Where should it go?"

"Sooner or later, if two people want to be with each other, they'll think of getting married or some similar type of commitment and live together. They need to merge their lives, their futures; you know, start a family."

"I've been thinking of that!"

"Perhaps, but Hans hasn't."

"How do you know that?"

"Has he ever asked you to marry him?"

"Well, no, but..."

There, you see, those are not his thoughts. If he thought of you as more than just a girlfriend, he would have married you a long time ago!"

"But he's so busy with the Resistance and all that."

"You're just rationalizing. Life goes on! You can put your feelings and plans on hold only for so long. Eventually, no matter what, you must move forward, or life will pass you by.!"

"I think life is passing me by."

"And life is also passing by for Hans." He loves you as a good friend, but he needs more. He might just have found someone who can be more to him than you've been. I think you're seeing that. You and Hans have a good friendship, but it lacks the fiery passion that could take it to the next level, a higher level where you feel you cannot live without each other."

"Are you saying that we don't have what it takes to have such a relationship?"

"No, I am saying that your relationship doesn't have that kind of passion. I'm not saying that either of you are not capable of it, but the two of you together do not have it. You are too different from each other; different in a way that does not produce the spark necessary to ignite the passion required for the higher level. I think you know what I mean!"

"In other words, Hans may see something in Rachel he doesn't see in me. Is that the gist of it?"

"Yes, he may do more than just "see something" in Rachel, he may "feel" a lot of that "spark." He may finally have found the right person for him, a person that can truly ignite that passion in a big way. But you've yet to find that person for yourself."

"So, you're saying that Hans is not the one for me."

"I'm afraid that's right."

"Life is not just passing me by; my life is falling apart," Ulla said, starting to cry.

"I know all this is disappointing for you, but try to look at it this way. Better to have learned all this now, than waste more years yearning for what will never be. Think of it as a new beginning, where your life can take a new direction. A direction that can find the right person for you!"

"Those are wise words, Papa," Ulla whimpered, "where did you ever find them?"

"Oh, I've been around this planet for a long time. Besides, "Father always knows best", you know!"

Ulla had nervously been nibbling at the pastry as she drank her coffee. Now she slowly got up and left the table to go out for a walk on the beach. She began to think again.

Her Dad was right; her life did need a new direction.

But what would it be? What could it be?

No, what was important was what she wanted it to be!

After a long walk on the beach, Ulla found a comfortable sand dune to sit on and stare at the gray waves with white froth on top. She was mesmerized by the continuous flow and roar of the waves.

They never stopped coming. They were like the sea of life; it always kept going. It was like cars on a long, long train, as long as the eye could see. It just kept on going. It was possible to stop and get off, but then the train would continue. So if you got off, it would leave you behind.

Who knows what it would be like and where it would be when you stepped back on, if you could. She had been off for quite a while. She had to step back on. Her rambling thoughts could have kept her out on the beach all night. She only came home because she was cold. It was close to midnight, and she was soon in bed. Emotionally exhausted, she fell into a deep sleep.

CHAPTER 15

It was 9 AM. The sun was shining brightly through her window, bringing a delicious warmth to her room. Ulla arose with a new sense of determination. This new day was like a new beginning of her life. After endless thinking the day before, she was still talking to herself.

I'm going to make one last try at holding on to Hans and see if he can possibly become a part of my world. I'm also going to make an effort to become a part of his world. I know I might fail, but I've got to make one last try before I put a life-long friendship to rest, and search for a new and different relationship. The first step will definitely be to bring Hans back into my world.

"Hans, are you up yet?" She called and asked in a chipper tone.

"Ulla, is that you?"

"Of course it's me. What're you up to today?"

"I'm going into Rønne later on to do some business. Why do you ask?"

"Just curious. And I also wonder if you could do me a great favor?"

"I'll be happy to try; tell me what I can do!" Hans answered dutifully.

"Could you possibly deliver a package for me?"

"Sure, but why don't you just send it by mail?"

"I could, but I need to make it a more personal delivery."

"Really?"

"Well, it's a package with some of my creations, paintings on glass and porcelain. I'm trying to promote them through a department store in Rønne.

"Oh, that sounds exiting. I'll stop by and pick it up on my way, OK?"

"Great, I really appreciate that."

"No sweat, see you later."

He'll do it! How can you not just love a guy like that?

Ulla thought. Hans is still alive for me. It's just like old times. Perhaps my plan is really going to work.

Ole and Rachel had just started to hang a couple of hundred herrings up on the racks, when a familiar voice interrupted.

"Hi guys!"

"Hi Hans!"

Rachel turned around and gave Hans a brief hug.

"What're you up to?" Ole asked.

"I've got some business in Rønne, and I'm taking a package with me for Ulla."

"That's nice of you," Ole said. "I think she's in the house right now."

"OK, so long now."

Hans chatted briefly with Ulla, gave her a hug, picked up the package and was soon out of sight, on his way to Rønne. He returned a few hours later and brought back a receipt and a letter for Ulla. As Ulla was busy opening the letter, Rachel popped her head through the door.

"Excuse me Hans, but I need to speak with you right away!"

"That sounds urgent," Hans said. "I'll see you later Ulla,"

He left the house with Rachel, much to Ulla's annoyance.

"What's up?" He asked as they were out by the herring smokers.

"Wait, let me make sure no one's around," Rachel cautioned, as she looked around. "No, Ole has gone in; we're OK."

"Why all the secrecy?"

"I need to tell you about something I saw this morning," Rachel continued.

"What's that?"

Rachel lowered her voice almost to a whisper as she drew closer to Hans.

"Around noon today I saw what looked like a Nazi official in civilian clothes go into a house down the street a ways."

"A Nazi in civilian clothes? What makes you think it was a Nazi?"

"He drove a gray-green car with a strange license plate, definitely not a Danish one."

"Was he wearing a hat or a cap?"

"No, nothing like that."

"Was he carrying anything, like a briefcase or papers?"

"No, but he was wearing a long coat."

"What kind of coat?"

"Could be a trench coat!"

"Leather?"

"No, just heavy cloth with those little things on the shoulders and a belt."

"That's a trench coat."

"The Nazi rang the door bell and was let in by a tall thin man with a short black beard."

"How were you able to see all that?"

"I had just finished work and was coming in for lunch, when I saw the car go by. I stood behind the bush by the door and watched. What do you think?"

"I think you did a great job of observing all that and to remember so much. I think I've got a very good picture of it all. It sounds like a Gestapo officer to me. He was probably looking for evidence."

"Evidence? Of what?"

"Refugees."

"Oh my Gosh! Could that be evidence of me being here?"

"No, no. Only our families know who you are, so don't you worry!"

"But maybe he suspects something."

"Undoubtedly, but I'm more concerned about him talking with someone here in town, talking with someone that could be one of our very own residents!"

"Do you know the man he talked to?" Rachel asked.

"The man with the beard?"

"Yes."

"I think I've seen him walk along the shore, but I don't know who he is or what he does. He could be a painter, you know, an artist. We have a number of artists living right here in Tejn, but not all are year long residents."

"What does it all mean?"

"I'm afraid it's rather serious."

"How so?"

"Well, a visit like that during the day by a single Nazi in civilian clothes smells more like a secret mission of a higher level than a mere so called fishing expedition done by soldiers in uniform. That means that there has been prior contact, and that something valuable is being exchanged or arranged."

"Valuable? Like what?"

"Information."

"Come on Hans, don't be so secretive!"

"Probably information about the refugees. The bearded man must have seen something recently and decided to report it to the Nazis."

"To the Nazis?"

"He most likely will sell it to them, if he hasn't already."

"You mean he would actually rat on his own people for money?"

"I'm afraid so."

"What a scoundrel! Damned traitor!"

"It's hard to imagine any other reason for such a visit; but we'll need to investigate this immediately."

"He could've put the whole operation in danger," Rachel said.

"Absolutely, we must find out what he has seen and what he knows."

"And who that Nazi was," Rachel added.

"Exactly."

"OK...So do you want me to pay him a visit?"

"No, that would be much too dangerous for you. He may already know who you are!"

"But you just said no one knows who I am except for you and Ole's family."

"I know I said that, but now we know that he probably has seen or heard something, and that could include information about you."

"Oh great! Well, what better way to find out than for me to look him directly in the eye and see how he reacts!"

"You sure are ready for action, aren't you!?

"You bet. We can't let this go on for long."

"No, of course, but it might be better if I could keep an eye on his movements when he goes out, and see if I can get some more clues."

"Yeah, you can do that, but you know what I'm gonna do? I'll walk around in my work clothes and a head wrap, carrying a tray of smoked herring and offer people a taste. I'll walk up and down the street here; and that'll give me a chance to meet the guy, look him in the eye, and look inside, if I can. I could try to go inside and set my tray down somewhere and chat a while. I could then see if he has papers or other interesting items around. What do you say?"

"And let you walk right into the Lion's Den armed with a smoked fish?" Hans started to laugh. "You're crazy!"

"What could be a better disguise?"

"Actually, you may be right. You may have a good idea there. In fact, it's really a great idea!"

"Well?"

"It's just that I don't like you flirting with danger!"

"Yeah, I know. You would rather that I flirt with you, right?"

"You got that right!"

"Hey, I can take care of myself! Remember, I'm a freedom fighter now. And let me carry a pistol just in case."

"OK. If you get into a problem, I'll be close by. And if you're armed, you'll have a fighting chance. He may be armed, but I doubt it, unless he's also a Nazi."

"Yeah, I think we have to count on that possibility," Rachel said.

"I know a lady that lives right across the street from that house. She was a fishwife, but a widow now. She hates the Nazis. She'll let me stay in her living room a few days if I need to, so I can keep an eye on the 'Beard'!"

"Great! Keep an eye on me too please."

"Oh I will, but remember, avoid any confrontation at all cost. We don't want our little town swarming with Nazis all of a sudden!"

"Don't worry, I'll be real nice to him."

"Let's go in and tell Ole about your plan. I think the owner should know his assistant is out giving away his precious fish, don't you?"

"I might sell a few, you know!"

"Good!"

CHAPTER 16

The bearded man lived in a pink house on the south side of the street behind the harbor area. Right across the street, while unseen, Hans chatted with Mrs. Andersen, but able to observe the pink house through the sheer curtains draped across the living room window.

"Do you think this man is a Nazi?" Mrs. Andersen asked.

"At this point I don't know who he really is, but he could well be a Nazi spy, or worse yet, a Nazi collaborator," Hans replied.

"That's terrible! To have someone like that living right across the street! Do you suppose he could be watching me, like looking into my living room with binoculars?"

"I doubt that he's just a Peeping Tom watching you with his binoculars. We could easily deal with that."

"Yeah, take him out back and give him a good thrashing!"

"There you go! But it sounds to me like he's giving information to the Nazis about something he may have observed here in town."

"You mean he's a spy?"

"No, more like he's an informer."

"Oh my, that's worse. Then he's a traitor, isn't he?"

"Yes. Oh, look there, he's going out. I think I'll follow him," Hans said, as he immediately went toward the door.

The bearded man walked casually toward the harbor, wearing a black beret and carrying a small canvas and a palate with paints and brushes. Hans followed equally casually a good distance behind. There was no one around, as the fishermen were still sleeping, after being out at sea during the night. The bearded man walked toward the pier and strolled slowly out to the end of it, while scouring the ground right and left. He stood several minutes at the end of the pier and studied the shore line.

Hans had retreated behind the edge of a house and remained unseen. The man took out his canvas and started to paint, while standing at the tip of the pier.

After painting a few strokes, he tucked his canvas away and left. Most artists will want to spend a little time, while on a location, sitting down and making the most of their time. This man's brief appearance seemed a bit odd. It looked like he came away empty handed, but had made a few paint strokes on his canvas to support his business there as a painter. Hans hurried back to Mrs. Andersen's house and described what he had seen.

"Well, what do you think? Mrs. Andersen asked.

"I'm not sure if he really is an artist, or what I saw was just a disguise? Perhaps he's looking for a good observation spot, where he can spy on the activities in the harbor.

As if on cue, he appeared at the top of the street and soon went into his house.

"What now?" Asked Mrs. Andersen.

"We have a plan, and I think it's about to unfold. Just keep watching the street."

At that moment, Rachel was coming down the street with a large tray of golden brown smoked herrings, giving samples to several people.

She arrived at the pink house and rang the door bell.

There was no response.

She rang again.

A window shade moved slightly.

Finally the door opened.

The bearded man stared at Rachel without saying a word. Apparently he had never seen a large tray of smoked herrings with a girl attached.

Rachel began an enthusiastic conversation with the poker faced bearded man.

Without saying a word, he started to close the door.

Rachel made a few violent gestures with her free hand, pointing to the inside of the house.

It seemed forever before the man finally retreated.

He let her come in.

The door closed behind them.

The street was empty and quiet once more.

"She got inside!" Mrs. Andersen erupted in surprise.

"I wish I could hear what they were saying," Hans said.

"Is this really your plan?"

"Yes, it's all going exactly as planned."

Ten minutes went by.

Not a sound could be heard.

"I hope she's all right in there," Hans fretted.

Just then the door opened, and Rachel emerged from the pink house.

She cast a brief smile in the direction of Mrs. Andersen's house and proceeded further down the street, ringing the next door bell.

Both Hans and Mrs. Andersen drew a sigh of relief.

Rachel was OK.

Mission accomplished!

"Rachel, how did you ever manage to get inside? It looked like he was going to shut the door right in your face!" Hans asked.

"I know, I thought so too. But let me start at the beginning. By the way, all the people I talked to were absolutely delighted to get free samples of the main product of Tejn. The free stuff really got their attention. That in itself just made my day! Then when I met the bearded man, it was the complete opposite. He was absolutely grouchy and extremely impolite, the way he just stood there and stared at me menacingly. He talked softly, and I could hardly hear what he said under his beard. But it sounded like he said he detested fish, and he had to get back to his work. He started to close the door, and I thought it was all over. I realized I'd better make a desperate attempt to get in. It was now or never, so to speak."

"I had to make one last try to change his attitude. I almost screamed at him that if he lived in this little town, the least he could do was to support the local businesses, especially since he would probably expect the same support for his business. You're an artist aren't you," I said. "You want people to buy your paintings don't you? That means they'll have to look at your paintings first don't they? Well, here, look at these smoked herrings! Do you see how they have a rich golden brown color. Surely as an artist like you can appreciate such a unique and vibrant color, can't you? They've been changed! They taste totally different, like nothing you've ever tasted before! Here, let me just set my tray down on your table for a moment, my arm is really getting tired. I'll show you. This is truly a national culinary treasure! You must be able to see that! Do you know that all the other people on the street were delighted to get a few samples absolutely free?

Then he actually changed his mind!

I guess he didn't want to appear out of place with the rest of the people in town. Or maybe he was just getting tired of me being there and just wanted to get rid of me."

"That was spectacular Rachel! What happened then?"

"I saw a typewriter on his table; so I tried to set my tray down as close to that as I could. I was then able to cast a quick glance at the paper he was typing, and in that fraction of a second I saw a small fragment of a sentence that seemed to jump off the page at me."

"Yes, yes, what was it? Don't keep me in suspense."

"All I saw was 'Refugees out of Tejn' in big letters."

"Wow! That was enough! You've discovered an informer!" Hans exclaimed. "Go on."

"I opened a herring and scooped out a piece of the fillet and handed it to him. He took it reluctantly, then tasted it gingerly, like he might throw up. Then surprise! He said he liked it! He accepted two whole herrings and thanked me. That's when I thought I'd better get out while the going was good. I picked up my tray and left. I almost became speechless, when I saw what was written on the typewriter.

But whatever, I got in!

And what's even better, I got out again!

Here I am unscathed. How do you like that?"

"You were fantastic! Absolutely incredible!"

"Hey, this was fun. I'll have to do this again some time.

It's amazing how many people pay little attention to Tejn's major resources; but the free fish really woke them up. That's just what Ole needs at this slow time for all businesses."

"Good idea. I'm sure Ole will be happy for that. But now we have a serious problem on our hands. We have an informer or traitor that has observed something, perhaps even the actual secret boarding of refugees late at night and the departure of the fishing boat with them."

"What now?"

"We must intercept that paper. It's obviously intended for the

Nazis. If they receive that, our little town of Tejn will be swarming with Nazis, and the escape program will be over."

"It's pretty serious isn't it?"

"I'm afraid so. Both the paper and the bearded man must be eliminated."

"When and how?"

"Now!"

That word sent a chill down Rachel's spine. She was game on almost anything, even actual combat. But what was about to happen sounded like a planned lethal attack, not a surprise encounter and skirmish with the Nazis. This would be a planned taking of a life, that of a civilian local resident, a Dane no less. At least he is assumed to be a Dane.

"What if he really is a painter and is just writing a letter to his family?"

"Yeah, the Nazi official's family!"

"Don't you have any doubts about who he is and what he's really doing?"

"No. I have no doubt that he is a traitor, and that he's about to destroy the opportunity for hundreds of Jewish refugees to be rescued. The paper he's about to deliver to the Nazis prove that. There's also no doubt that he and the letter must be stopped."

"Can't he be arrested and just go to jail?"

"By whom? The Nazis have confiscated our police force and sent them to concentration camps in Germany. We have no one to arrest traitors, and no jails in which to keep them. Besides, it's a capital offense."

"Then the Danish Resistance has become the judge, jury and executioner all wrapped up into one, hasn't it?"

"Yes, it's all we have right now. But it works.

It works because we make it work. It's justice and survival combined. It's swift. It's instant justice!"

"What an awesome responsibility to have," Rachel said.

"It takes strong shoulders," Hans replied. "It takes people like you and me. People that are idealists, honest, as well as practical and capable of fighting for our values. We'll not be corrupted by anyone or anything. We're a free people and we'll always fight to stay free. We'll preserve justice for our people as best we can without a police force. We're not a vigilante group or a lynch mob; we're calm and dedicated freedom fighters sworn to protect our people from the biggest threats to them right now, traitors and Nazis.

"Have you ever been face to face with a traitor?"

"No, I never have, and it's true what you say Rachel, that there's quite a difference between taking the life of a traitor compared to taking lives in a combat situation. The latter is a situation that forces you to decide between death of the enemy or your own death. There is no choice there! It's simply a matter of survival. Instant survival vs. instant death. They're shooting at you.

"No doubts there!"

"But traitors are very sneaky. They can't afford to leave a trail of evidence behind them. It's just like a murder mystery. You know who the murderer is, but you can't prove it. Here I know who the traitor is, but I can't prove it. Yet!

"How can you do that?"

"I need to force him to show his hand somehow.

I'm OK with taking one life to save many lives.

But I have to be absolutely sure that the life I take really is the guilty one.

My fear is always that I might make a mistake."

"It takes courage to do something like that."

"That's right. I have to overcome the instinctive restraint on taking a human life. Even though it's quite clear that the traitor must die, it's still a monstrous ethical problem."

"But how can you be absolutely certain that he really is a traitor?"

"That's what I'm saying. I have to verify that first!"

"And how exactly do you do that?"

"I've got it!" He shouted out loud, "I'll get the traitor to incriminate himself. In the absence of gathering evidence for a trial by jury, self incrimination remains the only absolute method of verification. Here's what I'll do. I'll pose as a Nazi messenger sent by the island Kommandant in Rønne to collect the written report by the local observer (collaborator). I have to see the contents of that report before the Nazi officer returns and gets his hands on it. I also have to see it before the bearded man can relay the information by telephone to Nazi headquarters in Rønne. You know, I actually have no time to lose. I have to go there immediately."

"What'll you do if you verify that he really is a traitor? What then? You can't just take him out on the street and shoot him in broad daylight, or can You?"

"No, that's the Nazi way of doing things; and shooting him in his house would soon be discovered. That would cause difficulties for the whole town."

"Perhaps you could wait till the evening?"

"Yes, then I could take him out to sea with a fishing boat. There I could give him a choice, a bullet or the deep blue sea."

"Not much of a choice."

"No, but at least it would be known that the man had had one last choice, his last choice on this planet."

I'll go there now to confirm my suspicions and hold him there till after dark."

Hans went by the harbor to alert Nils that he had to go to sea on a mission of justice after dark.

"I'll come by there in a little while," Nils agreed.

"Great, see you then."

CHAPTER 17

Hans went home and donned an old German uniform, strapped on his pistol and took his bike over to the pink house.

He rang the door bell.

No answer.

He knocked heavily on the door.

An eye peeked out between the edge of the window shade and the window frame.

The door opened.

He was led inside.

Hans raised his right arm and began in fluent German.

"Heil Hitler! Haben Sie den Bericht?" (Heil Hitler! Do you have the report?)

"Yes, it's right here," the man answered, not returning the greeting, "but may I ask who you are?"

"Ich bin Kapitan Schröder aus Rønne Abteilung."

"I don't understand. Why are you then wearing a soldier's uniform?"

"Look here, this soldier's uniform is only a disguise. I am on a secret mission. You see if this report is as urgent as I think it is,

I cannot permit wasting time to travel to Headquarters. I shall telephone the vital information immediately. Understand?"

"Yes, yes Hr. Captain." The man handed Hans an envelope.

Now Hans needed to know whether the information had managed to find its way back to the Nazis before they would get the written report.

"Haben Sie schon den Kommandant telefoniert?" (Have you telephoned the Kommandant yet?)

"No, but I will, now that the report will be on its way there."

That was it!

The man just implicated himself by declaring his intention to telephone the Nazi headquarters and reveal the contents of the report he had just prepared.

Now there was no way out.

This traitor had to be shot, unless he chose instead to die in the sea. Now, Hans needed to know if any information had been revealed to anyone else up to now.

"Have you told anyone else about your observations?"

"No, not yet, but I'll telephone headquarters this afternoon."

Now came the tricky part of disarming the man before he had a chance to use one of the many weapons he might have hidden around.

"This report may cause quite a lot of unrest in the population up here. Have you been wise enough to protect yourself by keeping a weapon up here?"

"Yes, of course!"

"What kind of weapon do you have?"

"A pistol."

"Like this one?"

Hans drew his pistol from the belt holster and pointed it to the right side, so as not to be perceived as confrontational.

"No, it's smaller."

"You'd better let me check it. It would not be good for you if it were too small. You know what I mean!"

Without answering, the bearded man opened a slim drawer under the tabletop and removed a medium sized automatic pistol, a 9mm Browning.

"Let me see that!" Hans demanded with a hint of doubt in his voice.

"You won't take it will you? The man asked with sudden fear and distrust of Hans' intentions.

"No, I prefer my own, but yours is good too."

The man handed his pistol to Hans, who examined it for corrosion around the mouth of the barrel. He also in a concealed fashion pressed the button that released the clip with bullets so it silently popped out a fraction of an inch.

"A bit of corrosion in the barrel. You should clean it better," Hans said casually.

He lay the pistol back down on the table, but right in front of himself, a far reach across the table from the bearded man.

With a fingertip he held on to the clip and removed it from the gun, keeping it covered by his withdrawing hand.

"Before I leave," Hans said, "I need to check this report, and I may have to telephone the Kommandant from your telephone right now."

"But this report is only for the Kommandant; no one else is allowed to open it!"

The man was suddenly very concerned and remained standing across the table from Hans. He stared at Hans with a very confused and bewildered look. It seemed a bit odd to him that an officer would need to come in a disguise. Furthermore, why was he so intent on saving an hour's time in this matter? Surely an hour would make no difference, especially since the report would probably just sit on a desk for no less than several hours. Well, it was not for him to judge. He had done his observations and put them in writing in the report, so now the Nazis could handle it in any way they wished. Still, he did not trust the Nazis.

He felt very uneasy that his pistol had wandered from its secure position in the drawer in front of him all the way up and across the table to lie in front of this supposed Nazi officer, nearly out of his reach no less.

While keeping his finger on the trigger of his pistol, holding it just under the paper, Hans opened the envelope and started to read the report. It described in great detail the observation of groups of people boarding a fishing boat at midnight, and then the boat leaving the harbor. Hans also saw the words "Refugees out of Tejn" that Rachel had seen. They were part of a clear description of the escape:

Several fishing boats were taking refugees out of Tejn harbor at midnight and headed for Sweden with them.

There followed a list of suspected people that were involved with that whole operation. He read the list:

Hans	Captain Jay
Nils	Mark
Ole	Dr. Levi
Rachel	

Hans had now verified that the escape program had been discovered. He had also verified that the man was a collaborator, and that he was armed. He had implicated himself by writing the report, arranging for it to reach Nazi Headquarters in Rønne and stating clearly that he was about to telephone Headquarters with the information contained in the report.

Hans had seen and heard enough.

Up until now, the logic of the facts had been well perceived and understood by Hans for many hours now. But seeing the actual evidence, and standing face to face with the traitor caused his emotions to finally catch up. He became increasingly angry and incensed at the despicable traitor standing in front of him.

He reacted out of emotion rather than logic.

He subconsciously inflamed the emotions of the traitor, in order to incite him to react in a way that would justify immediate execution.

He subconsciously wished for him to try to reach across the table for his weapon, which of course would justify instant lethal force. Or would it?

It would if Hans didn't know the gun was unloaded.

The only problem was that he did know it was unloaded, having just unloaded it himself. Therefore no justification! He instantly realized what he had thought, and wisely decided not to pursue that course of action.

He quickly returned to reality. He decided to see what else the man might be able to disclose or do voluntarily.

"Look here, this report is highly inflammatory. It may well start a revolt by the people! It needs to be destroyed at once!" Hans exclaimed.

"But Hr. Captain, that is not for you to judge!"

"What do you suggest?" Hans asked.

The man perceived that question as a moment of weakness, allowing him to voice an objection.

He immediately seized the moment in a last ditch effort to control the situation. He suddenly reached far across to the other side of the table and retrieved his pistol, cocked it and held it ready to fire directly at Hans.

"Give me that report, or I'll shoot!" He shouted.

"Did you hear me? If you don't hand over that report immediately, I shall be forced to shoot you!"

He was becoming more desperate, as Hans remained calm. Hans didn't say a word, nor did he move a muscle.

"Very well, have it your way!" The man warned.

A click was heard.

The man looked up in disbelief.

"I took the liberty of removing the bullets from your pistol," Hans said calmly. You have just proved that you would have shot me, and that makes you my enemy. Now, put your hands up and turn around!" Hans commanded, while pointing his pistol directly at the man. The man became white as a sheet, but obeyed.

"Drop the gun!" Hans continued.

"Please Captain, please, I am the one who wrote the report, remember. I provided all the information. All that valuable information! Have I not done a good job? I was going to telephone Headquarters immediately after you had ......"

Hans didn't want to hear anymore.

He struck a hard blow to the top of the man's head with his pistol. The man fell instantly to the floor, still holding his pistol. Hans returned his own pistol to its belt holster, then replaced the clip with bullets into the man's Browning pistol and put it in his pocket. He removed the man's belt and secured his hands behind his back, then dragged him into his bedroom and wrapped a blanket around his head.

He went over to the table and pulled out the drawer to see what other evidence of treason there might be. His eye caught an official looking envelope. He opened it. It was stuffed with twenty large bills of 500 Danish Kroner each, a total of 10,000 Kroner. He put the money in his pocket. Way in the back of the drawer there was another envelope. It contained a handwritten report of some kind. Hans scanned through it. It listed all the drop sites for weapons and supplies from England to the Danish Resistance in the past several months.

It noted the frustration over the fact that they were all discovered too late to catch any of the Resistance members, but that he was close to discovering how to find out ahead of time, by intense surveillance of people on a long list from Tejn and surrounding towns.

He and Nils were on that list! Now he had further evidence that this man was a deadly traitor.

He was just about to go out and bring his bike in behind the house, when the door bell rang.

Hans pulled the Browning pistol out of his pocket and went over to the door. It didn't really matter who it was, he could not avoid answering the door bell.

If it were the Nazi officer returning, that would be just too bad for him. He would be too late to get what he would have come for, and he would walk right into his own death. Hans was hoping that it would be somebody else.

Anybody else!

Please, anybody else.

He didn't want to shoot anyone at this time of night.

He opened the door.

Another bearded man arrived.

It was Nils, his good fisherman friend!

"Hey, thanks for coming so quickly," Hans said.

"That's OK, what's happening? Nils asked.

"This man is a Nazi collaborator, and I have all the evidence I need. The man is knocked out and tied up in the bedroom. We just have to get him down to the boat. Did you bring the cargo-bike?"

"Yeah, I got it out back."

"Great, let's get on with it."

It had been dark for an hour or so. There was no one on the streets; they were all busy eating dinner. Hans and Nils carried the bearded man, still out cold, out the back door and placed him in the shallow box-like cargo bay of the cargo bike. Without turning on the bicycle lanterns, both men quickly made their way to the pier and brought the man on board. They placed him in the secret hiding place and closed the cover. Nils looked around, saw no one, and decided to cast off.

Far out in the Baltic north of Bornholm, the sea was peaceful with two foot waves rolling in from the West. At about twenty miles off shore, the tranquility was broken by a thumping noise coming from the locker. The man had come to and didn't like his surroundings. He was kicking the cover to the hiding place to get attention. Nils removed the cover and pulled him out. Hans unwrapped the blanket from his head and sat him on a crate in front of the pilot house. The man looked around in complete disbelief.

"Where am I?" He muttered.

"You're out on the deep blue sea," Nils answered.

"How did I get here?"

"We brought you out here," Hans answered.

"Who are you?"

"We're the Danish Resistance!" Nils said.

His eyes widened and his mouth dropped open. He realized he had been found out, and was now in deep trouble.

"My name is Nils, and this is Hans, our fearless leader," Nils continued.

"What do you want with me?"

"We want justice," Hans said.

"What does that mean?"

"It means that you'll have to pay for your crimes."

"What crimes?"

"Do you recognize this report?" Hans asked as he pulled out the report the man had typed.

The man suddenly became silent.

"How about this one?" Hans pulled out the hand-written one.

The man remained silent. At this point he had no doubt that all his activities had been discovered, and this whole encounter could only end in his death.

"Let me refresh your memory. I came to your house in a Nazi uniform this afternoon, and this is the report you handed me to take to Nazi Headquarters. I can recite further evidence against you, evidence that you are a traitor; but that won't be necessary, as your silence has betrayed you. You're going to pay for your despicable crimes with your life, so that many others will be free to live. We call that justice. You'll have a choice between two bullets from our guns, or the deep blue sea right over there. If you refuse to choose, the choice will be made for you. But since we won't know your preference, and since we don't wish to deny you your preference, you'll be given both choices combined," Hans concluded.

The man became white as a sheet, but remained silent. He knew he was doomed at the hands of two top Danish Resistance fighters, who called a spade a spade.

"Tell us your name," Nils asked.

"My name is Karl."

"Are you Danish?" Hans asked.

Again the man said nothing.

"Again your silence betrays you." Hans said.

"But I didn't do anything!" He pleaded, his voice cracking.

Those were the last words that Hans wanted to hear at this time. Had he not been so thorough in establishing the man's guilt, his conscience might have been rattled, and a lot of time would have been wasted in putting on a trial at sea. But Hans continued unabated.

"You have identified yourself as a traitor by acknowledging that you made observations about places and people here in Tejn and wrote not just one report but two reports about all that, and then you sold them to the Nazis. That would have cost many innocent lives, if I hadn't intercepted them. You have sold out your own countrymen for money. You have been found guilty of Treason and Collaboration with the enemy. You have sixty seconds to make your choice: Bullets or the Sea!" Hans had finished.

Both Nils and Hans drew their pistols and aimed them directly at the traitor.

There was dead silence for sixty seconds.

Two shots were heard.

The dead Traitor was thrown overboard into the Baltic Sea and sank rapidly, reaching his own level at the bottom. Traitors have always been considered the lowest forms of human life; this one soon reached his level on the planet, the bottom of the sea.

The mission of justice was over.

The Danish Resistance had removed a serious threat to themselves, the refugees and the general population.

They had insured that their critical life saving work was able to continue.

Hundreds of lives had been saved!

CHAPTER 18

Ulla was far from pleased with Rachel's impressive performance, both as a Resistance member as well as a business woman. She had single handedly verified that the bearded man in the pink house was a traitor, as well as run a highly successful marketing campaign for Ole's smoked herring business.

"Absolutely incredible!" Ulla said, as she consulted her Dad. "Rachel not only had the brains to devise such a plan; but she also had the courage to carry it out, all by herself no less! One little slipup, and she could've been killed!"

"Not bad for a newcomer," Ole remarked.

"Is she completely naïve and oblivious to such risks, or is she really that courageous?"

"I'm afraid she's really both smart and very courageous," Ole said.

"Now, why couldn't I have thought of all that?"

"Maybe you could have, or maybe you're just not cut out to be a Freedom Fighter."

"What do you expect from a girl in a small country town? I mean, I just don't have the courage for that sort of thing."

"What's worse, you may also not have the business savvy that Rachel does."

"I just do my work. I know I'm good at what I do."

"But it takes more than that to have a successful business," Ole advised.

"Well, if all I can do is work at something, all I am is a worker, an employee, working for somebody else.

I'll always be told what to do and how to do things.

To rise above that, to the next higher level, where I work only for myself, where I can decide everything for myself, where I can determine my own destiny, good or bad, I am going to have to make a change."

"You're absolutely right, and to rise to that level, where you decide everything, you need to be able to promote your work effectively. You need to let the world know you exist!"

"Well, maybe just Bornholm."

"No, the world sounds better! You need to let the world know who you are, and what it is you want to sell."

"So, I need to advertise!"

"Yes, yes, yes!"

"That'll be a whole new ball game. I've never really had to think about that before."

"You gotta do what you gotta do!"

"But, just a minute now! You know what? I've already started to promote my business."

"What have you done?"

"I've just sent some of my art work to Rønne.

I'll just have to devote a lot more time and effort to that sort of thing. I've been a slow learner, but I'll catch up, you'll see. I feel both depressed and elated at the same time. It sounds weird, I know. How can I possibly feel two ways, two completely opposite ways at the same time?"

"How do you mean?"

"Well, I feel depressed over the fact that it was Rachel that was the star performer and not me. But at the same time, thinking about all that has made me suddenly see my shortcomings more clearly; and that enabled me to find the path forward. I now realize what it is I have to do to become more successful in my business. It's like a light coming on in my brain. Now I can see the way, and it gives me new hope. In fact, I'm truly elated at this discovery. I suddenly feel great. The good news seems to have outweighed the bad. I feel myself again, and I can think clearly again. I realize I'm already halfway there! I already own my own business. I'm my own boss. I'm not an employee. I have already risen to that higher level. Think of how many people have not done that yet! My cup's not half empty. It's half full!"

"Hold that thought," Ole said as he went out.

She called Hans to share her excitement with him.

His phone didn't answer. Where could he be, her imagination started to run again. I know he isn't out with Rachel; she's in her room reading.

Ulla went over to his house. No lights were on.

Is he sleeping? I'll go around back. Oh, oh; his bike is gone. He isn't home! He must be out on business.

Oh well, at least he's not out with Rachel.

CHAPTER 19

It was December, 1944.

The escape from Koszalin was in full swing, having moved nearly 2,000 Jewish refugees from Poland to Sweden. Nothing seemed to stop the flow of Jews to safety. Periodic boardings on the high seas, interrogations in the Ghetto, confrontations on the pathways across Bornholm – nothing stopped the determined escape of Jews to Sweden.

December set in with especially bad weather. Several severe winter storms ravaged the Baltic Sea and surrounding lands. The storms literally froze the efforts to transport people across the Baltic Sea. The fishermen could barely venture out to fish, much less complete the scheduled transport of people across the angry waves, high winds and pelting sleet and snow.

"Hans!" One of his compatriots said one evening, "We're running into a problem."

"What's that?"

We seem to have way too many refugees on the island at this time."

"Yeah, I've noticed there are a lot more refugees than usual; but you know, we haven't been able to send as many boats to Sweden lately because of the weather."

"Yeah, that's forced a lot of those people to stay in Tejn, not a good thing."

"How many do you think are waiting there now?"

"At least 50."

"What? That many?"

"Yeah, at least!"

"How can that be? If our boats can't go out, how can people be coming here on boats from Poland?"

"I think the Polish fishing boats may be a little bigger than ours. They brave the rough seas and just keep on coming."

"Wow! That shows you how desperate those people are!"

"Yeah, and the fishermen are incredibly courageous, taking on all sorts of risks."

"Well, they probably won't see many German patrol boats out there in these storms."

"You got that right, but what can we do about it? Next week we could have a hundred people here."

"It'll take quite a while to reduce that number using our regular boats, unless...," Hans paused a moment.

"Unless what?" His friend was getting very curious.

"Unless ... we could just find a larger boat!"

"What kind of boat would that be?"

"It'd have to be a small freighter or even a ferry boat."

"And just where do we get that?"

"We'll have to get one in Rønne

"Just like that?!"

"Hey, just think for a moment! Desperate problems require desperate solutions! Look at the big picture! There's nothing here that'll take 100 people to Sweden. There's nothing that'll get the job done other than a really big boat. So that's what we'll have to get!"

"It's a good thing you are so goal oriented!"

"It's the only way to fly!"

"OK, when do we start looking?"

"Right now! Let's go to Rønne and see what they've got in the harbor we can use."

Hans and his friend biked to Rønne immediately. It was the largest city on Bornholm, with approximately 12,000 inhabitants. A large central square was peppered with underground bomb shelters with gray saucer shaped tops, like space ships that had just landed. They arrived just before dark at the central town square, called "Store Torv" or "Big Square". They parked their bikes in an alley next to the town movie house and walked across the square toward the harbor.

"Do you remember when we were playing grocery clerks over there?" Hans pointed to the northwest corner.

"How could I forget? You almost got us killed."

"Oh, nonsense! It was about six months ago, and you were just inexperienced then."

Usually at least two or three German walking patrols of two soldiers each could be seen at any given time of day. One day close to noon, Hans and his friend were pushing a two wheeled cart full of dark brown granular material labeled artificial coffee. They were dressed with the usual white aprons worn by grocery clerks. As they neared the northwest corner of the square and were about to get lost in the crowd on that busy street, the wheel near the curb came off, and the cart nearly tipped over and spilled some of the brown material. Immediately two German soldiers came up.

"What are you doing?" They asked, like they had never seen a grocery delivery before.

"Just delivering some artificial coffee," Hans replied, as he jumped up on the brown material and lit a cigarette, casually throwing the match in the gutter, "Kaffe Erzatz!"

The German soldiers lost interest and moved on.

"Are you crazy? His friend asked frantically.

"No," Hans said, they don't know we're delivering gun powder! I had to do something to be convincing."

"But you could have blown us to kingdom come!"

"Ah, but I didn't. I made sure the match was out and cold before I threw it! Now let's get the wheel back on and get going."

"Yeah, Hans, that was a cool maneuver all right. But I also remember the massacre in the center of the Square."

"Yeah, that was an outrageous event."

Gun battles, or so called "fire fights" had become more frequent, as the resistance movement became more aggressive in destroying German equipment and arms. In a recent such gun battle, a German officer had been shot and killed. The Nazis did not take kindly to such outright armed rebellion and took revenge the next day. A typical "Goon Squad" roared into the Big Square at noon, and four soldiers and an officer jumped out of the military vehicle. They went around the square and arrested ten of the merchants, all men.

They proceeded to line them up in a straight line in the middle of the square. They then asked the impossible:

"One of our officers was shot and killed last night. Which one of you is responsible for that?"

No one said a word.

"Will the person responsible step forward immediately!"

No one moved. It probably was not one of the merchants from the square, although some were in the Resistance. But even if it had been one of them, the answer would have been the same. It was always the old French Three Musketeer principle, "All for One and One for All."

If it had been one of the merchants, his reluctance to step forward was only reasonable, in that it would not be long before he would be shot on the spot. The Nazis were good at being instant judge, jury and executioner.

If one of them had stepped forward, the others would undoubtedly have stepped forward in an attempt to save him by hoping to distribute the responsibility to all of them, thus suggesting a less violent punishment. And if they didn't all step forward, and one of their comrades was shot and killed, they would never be able to live it down; they would never be able to forgive themselves for not at least trying to save him by all stepping forward.

The impossibility of the situation was further complicated by the fact that the actual person that fired that fatal shot, very likely did not even know himself that he had fired that shot. It could well have been another shooter. Furthermore, he might not even know that his shot had felled an officer; he was only firing back at some Nazi shooting at him.

So who cared? Who cared whether it was a Nazi officer or a simple German soldier that got shot? The Resistance was not out specifically to kill people, even Nazis. They were only out to destroy the German military machine, or at least cripple it as best they could. That meant destroying equipment, vehicles, arms, ammunition, and most importantly, lists of freedom fighters, maps, plans of operations, orders from Nazi headquarters that all would have a direct impact on the safety and survival of Danish citizens.

In war, civilian people hurt or killed were labeled "collateral damage" and unfortunately come with the territory. Military personnel killed is part of war. The Germans had invaded Denmark, and now they were paying for it.

Such was the heavy burden of deep moral issues, all to be resolved in their minds in a few seconds. Indeed a heavy burden, an impossible task, a fatal task. The die was cast. Someone was about to die. It might as well be all of them, if they didn't do their best to intervene.

"If no one is willing to step forward, I shall be the one to pick someone to come forward.

Now, I ask you again, who is responsible for shooting a Nazi officer last night?"

Unbelievably, one merchant stepped forward.

Then a second.

And a third.

Soon all ten had stepped forward.

The Nazis were flabbergasted. How could the Danes make a mockery of their serious interrogation?

It was of course more like a "kangaroo court"!

"Very well then," the officer gasped. He continued,

"You leave me no choice!"

He employed the well known psychological defense mechanism of projecting the blame for what was about to happen over on someone else, thus believing himself to be free of responsibility.

"Get ready, aim."

The soldiers raised their rifles and aimed at the merchants.

The merchants braced themselves for what was totally unexpected.

The sudden death for all of them.

"FIRE!"

A series of gunshots rang out scattering spectators in all directions.

The ten merchants lay dead on the cobblestones of the square.

The Nazis mounted their vehicle and sped off quickly to avoid any reaction from the quickly growing crowd.

The bodies were quickly removed to a hospital morgue.

The blood on the cobblestones was not removed.

No one wanted to wipe out the evidence of what had just happened.

The blood stains would be a constant reminder of this Nazi atrocity.

The blood stains would remain until nature gradually wore them thin and eventually erased them.

They were not to be removed by human hands.

No Dane would dare touch them.

No Dane would want to touch them.

"That was truly a sad day for Denmark!" Hans said. I don't think any of us had any idea the Nazis could be so barbaric!"

"Barbaric is not the word! It was more than just barbaric.

It was truly Satanic.

Absolutely evil.

Evil beyond human understanding.

So vengeful, and to take it out on civilians!

It was all too much to bear.

After all these centuries of human conflict, won't man's inhumanity to man ever cease? They say that people that don't learn from the mistakes of history are doomed to repeat them. And as true as that may be, the Nazis must be aware of past atrocities, yet they seem to wallow in them themselves. What makes them do that? Is it really ignorance, or is it plain stupidity; or is it that the irresistible thirst for power and glory, like a sin of humanity, is too pervasive to ever be eradicated?" His friend speculated.

"Well, now we know what we're up against. So don't feel bad when we do what we have to do! Just remember that incident!" Hans returned to practicality.

"I'll never forget it," his friend added, " I don't think any one ever will."

As they walked across the Square, they stopped for a moment at the very site of the massacre.

"This is exactly where it happened," Hans said, as they both peered at the cobblestones in the center of the Square, "but I don't see any trace of that atrocity. Let's move on. It's only half a mile down to the harbor."

As they reached the harbor, the sun had set, and the overcast sky made for a brief twilight.

"I don't see any freighters," his friend said.

"Yeah, I just see two small fishing boats that look like they just came in with a good catch; they're unloading on the dock over there. Boy, this Harbor has grown since last year. I guess that's why it's able to serve a lot of fishing boats and private sailboats, as well as many freighters and ferries to Copenhagen and Malmö."

"What's that over there at the dock?"

"It looks like the stern of a large ferry."

"It's the "Hammershus"."

"Great, we're in luck! That's the ferry to Copenhagen.

It's named after the large medieval castle, now only ruins remaining. It's shaped like a small ocean liner with a large central smokestack, a high bow, and lots of small round ports.

The ship was docked along the edge of a wide cobblestone street that bordered the harbor. Various houses and pubs made up the other side of the street.

"Look, there's a German soldier walking back and forth near the railing aboard the ferry."

"Let's quickly go to the other side of the street by the houses and try to slip unseen into a local pub."

A few sailors were at the bar, and a man with a captain's hat was sitting alone at a small table nearby.

"Hi, are you by any chance the captain of the Copenhagen

149

ferry "Hammershus" out there?" Hans asked quietly as he pointed toward the door.

"That's right," came the terse reply.

"We want to go to Copenhagen. Can you tell us when you're sailing?"

"Yes, tomorrow night, 10 O'clock sharp. We'll be in Copenhagen at 6:00 AM the next morning. You can get your tickets right next door here tomorrow morning.

"Thanks a lot."

Hans and his friend left the pub and hurried off the waterfront.

"We've got little more than 24 hours to get all the refugees mobilized and brought here to the harbor."

"How do we do that? I mean, without the Germans discovering the refugees?"

"I have an idea," Hans said, "let's go."

"OK, so where're we going and what're we doing?"

"We're going to a phone booth on the Big Square and call our friends in Tejn who can lead all the refugees to Rønne harbor. Here's what they must do.

They must arrive in four groups late in the day. Across the street from the waterfront where the ferry is docked, there's a small warehouse with a large parking space behind it. Here the people can wait unseen, till they can be led aboard the ferry."

"You know what they said?" His friend whispered as they both emerged from the phone booths.

"What?"

"They said they were only too eager to go!"

"I'm not surprised! After all, here they're suddenly given a chance to travel on a regular ferry."

"Yeah, they're glad to travel in style; no more 'Sardines-in-a-can' fashion. They'll be like normal people."

"Except for one thing," Hans added. "This will be a high risk event. They'll trade comfort for high risk."

They didn't bat an eye.

"Have we not come through hell and high water already?"

"Has the Polish Resistance not protected us well?"

"Have the fishermen not risked their lives for us?"

"Has the Danish Resistance not been extraordinary?"

"Surely we'll be safe in the hands of the Danes!"

They were ready to go. Right now!

When Hans arrived back in Tejn, it was now ten o'clock at night. He visited several groups of people and prepared them for the journey to Rønne. There were no less than ninety people needing passage to Sweden. Hans arranged for two groups to go by the late afternoon busses, and another two groups to go by two early evening busses, all at different times.

"When the last group arrives at the warehouse lot, the people must be ready to quickly board the ferry," he instructed, "and have changed into Danish clothing. All religious head pieces can be worn provided they're covered by a hat or a cap."

At five o'clock the next afternoon, the groups began to arrive at the waterfront and gradually assembled behind the warehouse. At 9:45 PM, they were all led from the hiding place at the warehouse lot toward the ferry.

Not a word was spoken.

There was no smoking.

There was no laughter.

This was not a drill.

This was real life.

This was serious.

At five minutes to 10, Hans and his friend approached the gangway to the ferry. Only a few people were traveling that weeknight, and they'd all gone below to their overnight cabins.

The German guard stood at the opening in the railing as Hans approached, holding out one hand to grab the tickets and holding his rifle with the other hand. The rifle was slung over his right shoulder by a strap, but it was pointed right at Hans. Hans pulled out a couple of fake tickets and handed them to the guard.

As the guard reached for the tickets, Hans grabbed the barrel of the rifle with his left hand, ripping its strap off the guard's shoulder, and simultaneously landed a powerful right hand punch on the guard's nose, sending him backwards where his head struck the wooden deck.

His German helmet with its low sides covering the ears protected him from being knocked out, so Hans then struck a hard blow to his forehead with the butt of the rifle, after which the guard was out cold.

Hans gave the rifle to his friend, removed the guard's pistol from its belt holster and proceeded to the bridge or command center of the ferry.

His friend remained at the railing and shone a flashlight toward the warehouse and gave the green S.O.S. signal to the waiting leaders and refugees.

The refugees moved quickly toward the ferry and started to board.

Before the first refugee reached the ferry's deck, Hans's friend removed the German soldier to a closet inside a hallway, where he stayed locked up until in custody of the Swedish police.

Just as half of the refugees had crossed the street and were boarding the ferry, a sudden deafening engine revving noise signaled the arrival of a German motorcycle patrol heading right straight toward the line of refugees. It was the usual single seated motorcycle and a soldier in the sidecar with his rifle at the ready.

What now?

The Nazis were obviously annoyed at the street being full of people; and if they began to suspect anything, violent confrontation would be inevitable, and that would derail the whole escape plan.

While escorting so many refugees, the Danish Resistance did not take any chances and carried their home made machine guns under their long coats. But no one was looking for a fire fight in the street along the harbor. The patrol was now almost upon them and started to slow down.

"Let me have your scarf!" One of the Resistance members quickly grabbed a bright red scarf from one of the refugees and draped it diagonally across his chest front and back and tucked it in at the belt, front and back as well. He walked out into the middle of the street and held up his right hand, motioning the patrol to stop, With his left hand he waved the "passengers" on to continue crossing the street. It now seemed quite natural for all the "passengers" to board, as the ferry was ready.

The patrol stopped obediently, but obviously miffed at the sudden inconvenience. As soon as the last "passenger" had passed the roadway, the fellow with the red stripe turned and motioned to the patrol to pass. It wasted no time in thundering past and was soon out of sight in the darkness of the harbor.

Another close shave!

A touch of Danish instant ingenuity saved the night.

Once on the bridge, Hans greeted the captain, who recognized him from the night before.

The captain was rather cool.

"Good evening, Sir, but passengers are not allowed on the bridge. I must ask you to leave immediately. We're about to sail."

"That's all right, Captain, you see, I'm in command now!" Hans said calmly as he pulled out his newly acquired pistol and pointed it directly at the captain. The young helmsman could only stand motionless at the nearby wheel with his jaw dropping.

"What's the meaning of this? Guard!" He shouted.

"The meaning's very simple," Hans replied calmly. "You're going to take us all to Sweden! Oh, and don't worry about your guard, he's sleeping now, under lock and key."

"I can't change ports now!" The captain protested.

"Can't or won't?"

"I'm under orders!"

"By whom? The Shipping company or the Nazis?"

"It doesn't matter, I can't disobey my orders!"

"Look Captain," Hans got very serious. "I have by now 90 Jewish refugees aboard your ferry. They'll all be killed by the Nazis unless we get them to Sweden, NOW!"

"And what if I refuse?"

Was this man dense or what?

Could he be a collaborator with the Nazis?

Something was not quite right here.

Maybe he was just looking out for himself.

Not very patriotic, especially in a crisis such as this.

Well, whatever it was, time for discussion was over, and now it had to be handled with unmistakable force.

"I'm a Fisherman and a Pilot.

I'll take this ship to Sweden myself, right into Malmö harbor, with or without you. You will not like the part without you! Do I make myself clear?"

"All right, I'll do as you say."

"Cast off immediately, and do not fail to leave the harbor at your usual speed." Hans commanded.

"OK. Cast off!" He shouted to the deck hands on both bow and stern."Forward one quarter!" He telegraphed to the engine room, and the ferry edged slowly forward.

The helmsman gently turned the wheel toward the mouth of the harbor.

"Forward one half!" Was the next command from the bridge,

as the ferry was clear of the dock and had clear passage out of the harbor entrance. Once out of the harbor and into the two foot waves of the Baltic ocean, the captain commanded "Full speed ahead!"

The ferry soon reached its cruising speed of 15 knots, headed just off the wind by 20 degrees, setting its course for Copenhagen.

Six hours later, the ferry steamed up the seven mile wide waterway separating Denmark from Sweden called "Sundet" (The Sound).

"OK, now what?" The captain asked.

"When you're almost opposite the port of Malmö, make a 90 degree turn due East and follow the Copenhagen-Malmö ferry route all the way into Malmö harbor. Watch your speed. We don't want to arouse any suspicion."

"Very well!"

The captain followed the directions to the letter, and ten minutes after making the requested 90 degree turn toward Malmö, the ferry arrived in the harbor. The elated refugees had not dared sleep all night and were eager to disembark and get to a shelter.

The Swedish police were called and arrived shortly thereafter. They were quite surprised at the large number of refugees arriving with no prior notice, a veritable mob scene, and disembarking from a ferry, actually hijacked by the Danish Resistance. What will those Danes think of next?

The refugees were readily housed by the Swedes. The ferry was kept in Malmö for some time, as was the captain and crew. The German soldier was hospitalized for several weeks, then placed in a detention camp until further notice. Hans and his friend made their way back to Bornholm via a ferry from Eastern Sweden to "Gudhjem", a small fishing village on the north coast of Bornholm close to Tejn. They resumed their work as if nothing unusual had happened.

But actually something unusual had happened, and it changed the course of events.

CHAPTER 20

One week went by, and neither the ferry "Hammershus" nor its captain and crew had returned as scheduled to Rønne. It was not lost on the local German Headquarters that important ferry traffic had been disrupted. All patrols were questioned about anything unusual, but nothing was reported.

However, the motorcycle patrol that had to stop for the refugees also stated that they stopped for a long line of passengers boarding the ferry, but everything was peaceful and in order.

"Jah, Jah, Alles in Ordnung!"(Yes, yes, everything in order!) the patrolman said.

"Now just a minute," the officer insisted, "you say you had to stop for a long line of passengers boarding the ferry?"

"Yes, the ferry official was there, directing the traffic and stopping the cars and guiding the passengers across the street to the ferry."

"What ferry official? What traffic? What cars? There's no traffic there at night!"

"The official had a big red stripe over his black uniform."

"You Idiot! That was not a ferry official. There is no such thing. Did you see any cars? I doubt it, because there were no cars out there. And that long line of passengers was highly unusual, especially for a week night and should have caught your attention; and you should have reported it right away. It must have been a large group of Jews trying to escape from the island. Right under your noses! Stupid. Stupid. Stupid!" The officer fumed.

"But, Hr. Lieutenant, we thought the man with the red stripe was an official."

"Fools, both of you! Fools! You were both fooled by some guy in a dark coat obviously imitating some official, who knows who? You're dismissed. You will be taken off duty for an entire week. You know what you did? You let a hundred Jews escape from the island right under your noses.

Ach Du Lieber! (Oh, my Dear!)

What am I to do with such cub scouts?

Call the Naval Patrols in all Danish waters; no, the entire Baltic Sea! Tell them to intensify their search for escaping Jews." He finally finished his tirade, but didn't wait long before starting another one.

"Here we have a large group of refugees who were successfully transported to Sweden that night, and nearly went unnoticed, were it not for the fact that the ferry captain and crew were detained in Sweden, obviously on frivolous charges."

"Yes Hr. Lieutenant."

"It's clear that one thing has led to another, the missing guard at the ferry, missing captain and crew, disrupted ferry service, scattered reports by our spies in Sweden that several groups of Jews have begun to appear throughout Southern Sweden, and now the revelation by our motorcycle patrol that they saw a huge group of passengers boarding the Copenhagen ferry on a week night. It's starting to make sense, when you put all the pieces together. Why has it taken our intelligence more than a week to figure it out? Ridiculous!

Jews are escaping to Sweden right under our noses, and there doesn't seem to be anything we can do about it. We don't have a clue about where to start looking! Why not?"

"I don't know."

"Of course not! You know nothing! We have made absolutely sure we have everything under complete control, Jah? We have intensive efforts of interrogating, checking, boarding boats, threatening people all over, using dogs, shooting rebels, and oh, yes...also motorcycle patrols, ha, ha! How could anybody slip through all that? How? I'll tell you how! Because you imbeciles were on duty that night, that's how!"

The Nazis had overlooked one thing, and thereby had made one mistake! A big mistake!

In any confrontation, especially in war, mistakes are always very critical. This was driven home by a little story from the other side of the world, from the war in the Pacific, where Americans were fighting the Japanese.

After an American bombing mission, nearly all planes returned safely to their aircraft carriers, even though some had been damaged and straggled in late.

One such plane had part of its wing blown off by antiaircraft fire and was barely able to make it back. The pilot circled around a few times, looking for his carrier, then finally dropped down and approached the carrier deck quite correctly, touching down a little wobbly with the remaining wingtip scraping along the deck, sparks flying everywhere. He gradually came to a stop in front of the watching captain.

He triumphantly flung the cockpit cover back so he could climb out of the plane. He jumped down onto the deck and approached the captain, who smiled and said in his unmistakable Japanese accent,

"Velly nice, velly nice, but American Flyer make ah WONN mistake!! Zis is Japanese aircraft carrier!"

Back across the globe in Denmark, the Nazis had also made just one mistake. And it was a big one!

The intelligence of their soldiers was no match for the intelligence, quick wit and resourcefulness of the Danish people. Time and time again, the Nazis were outwitted by the Danes, which eventually contributed to their loss of control of their occupation of Denmark.

The Danish Resistance was quick to find the mental weakness of the Nazis and exploited it in any way they could.

The quick wit of the Danes was seen in this famous moment, when the Germans first occupied Denmark. The Nazis wanted very much to form a so called "coalition government", a combined government of the Danish Parliament and Nazi officials. It would've made German control of Denmark almost automatic.

When the Nazi delegation arrived at the King's Palace, they were ushered in to present the proposal to the King, who in Denmark has an important governmental role, approving elections, ministers, national and foreign policies. The King, a stately man in his seventies, listened attentively till they were finished. He then matter-of-factly told them:

"Gentlemen, it is my legs that are sick, not my head!"

The flabbergasted Nazis, unable to collect themselves from such a spontaneous and daring put-down, promptly left the palace, never to return.

So now the Nazis were to intensify their search for escaping Jews. Both the fishermen and the resistance groups had done an incredible job in executing all aspects of the escape plan. To be successful, it had to be perfect, and it was! Nevertheless, nobody was arrogant enough to think that it couldn't be even better, or that no re-evaluation would be prudent in the light of the impending new Nazi efforts. The news of the new Nazi attitude was quick to reach all the people involved with the plan, all the way back to Dr. Levi in Koszalin. Dr. Levi called another emergency meeting.

"Everything's gone so perfect, that we've had no need to meet like this." Dr. Levi began.

"I and all my people are truly grateful for all of your combined efforts and especially for the efforts of those daring fishermen and courageous resistance groups here and in Denmark. A million thanks to all of you!"

"When we meet like this again," he continued, "it's not because we have a problem anywhere, but it's to prevent any problems, now that the Nazis seem to be on to us. Obviously we have to be more careful than ever, and extra vigilant with everything we do. But the main thing we need to do is to develop a "plan B" for all the various links in the plan. For example, starting with the escape from the Ghetto, let us assume for the moment that one day the passes will be questioned and even revoked. What then? We must have a backup way to get the people out, a backup way to bring them to Darlowo, or perhaps change the boarding site to Mielno after all. Are there other boats than fishing boats that we could use? The Danes'll figure out their alternative plans, I'm sure."

"We'll be ready with all that in a couple of days," Mark said, "but tell us exactly what made the Nazis more aware of us than they already were?"

"I think it was the fault of the bad weather. That started the problem with delays, especially from Bornholm to Sweden over very rough waters. Soon there were too many refugees held up on Bornholm, and that was too dangerous, The Danes did a very brave and spectacular thing in high jacking that ferry to get them all out, but in so doing, the consequences conspired to increase the Nazi awareness of us. In other words, one thing led to another." Levi replied.

Dr. Levi was careful not to cast any blame on any individual or participants, as that would obviously be counterproductive. Everyone was doing his or her very best to get the job done.

"We don't have to meet again, but be sure to get word back to me about the backup plans," Levi said as he ended the meeting.

CHAPTER 21

It only took a few days back on Bornholm for Hans to realize that the Nazis were pretty upset over his latest caper. The news had spread fast that the Copenhagen ferry had been seized by a large group of Jewish refugees and taken to Sweden. That was OK with Hans, since it placed the blame and focus on the Jews, thereby leaving the Danish Resistance out of it. That gave the Resistance more room to operate, as they worked to help the refugees. However, Hans also realized that the heat would be turned up on searches on both land and sea. He decided to give the refugees armed protection.

"Hi, Nils. I heard you're not too happy about the need for armed protection, is that right?"

"Yeah, I think it'll take the whole program to a much higher level of risk. And who is going to wind up giving this armed protection and how?"

"Listen Nils, the program is already at a much higher level of risk. We'd only be adjusting our defenses accordingly. We'd be amiss not to do that. You know, if the refugees are discovered anywhere, on land or sea, they could be shot and killed on the spot. And even if they were just detained, it'd put an immediate stop to the whole escape plan. We simply could not continue in the same fashion. We' wouldn't have a safe course of action for any stage of the escape."

"Yes, I see that, but what good is armed protection really going to do?"

"Look Nils, if you're boarded out there, and the refugees are discovered, they'll be shot and thrown overboard; and what do you think'll happen to you? You'll likely be shot as well and your boat sunk!'

"We've done OK so far haven't we?"

"Yes, but that's because we've slipped by in the shadows. No one's suspected anything. But that's different now. It's caught their attention big time now that Jews are escaping, and right under their very noses!

They're incensed with outrage over it. They're highly embarrassed, and they'll do anything imaginable to find the refugees. They're like a trapped and cornered animal that'll lash out violently. They're insane with power and won't let go of what little they've got left. They won't let go until their last man is dead!

Don't you see? You won't stand a chance without arms!"

"I guess you're right; you always are! How do you get to know these bastards so well? How do you get inside their minds like you do?"

"I've lived under their boots long enough, and I've engaged them too many times not to know them inside and out. You know, the first rule of engagement is to know your enemy. That's a vital starting point. It doesn't matter whether it's a tennis match or a talent show, but also in a chess tournament where you must know your opponent across the board, and especially in war, where lives are at stake, knowledge of your enemy is imperative!"

"OK, so what do you want me to do?" Nils gave up.

"Here, take this Luger. It's still fully loaded. I didn't have to fire even a single shot. Remember, a threat is often more powerful than the action itself."

"Yeah, well that works best on the regular soldiers and traitors, but not on officers. They're more experienced and don't answer to threats."

"You're right, and that's why they must be handled with unmistakable force. They must be shot without hesitation."

"What does all that mean?" Nils didn't want to suddenly get confused by overwhelming information.

"It means that if the refugees are discovered, the boarding patrol must be shot dead instantly! Do not let them have a fraction of a moment to think, or you'll be shot first! You got that? Make it a reflex action. Refugees discovered – shoot to kill, officers first."

"OK, OK, I just wish it hadn't come to that."

"You and me both! But you know, the war is slowly coming to an end, with the advance of the allies on both fronts, and the Nazis are getting more and more desperate by the hour. When will you be ready for your next group?"

"Tomorrow night."

"OK, I'll try to get you another pistol, so you can have two. Two is always better than one."

"But where do I hide them?" Nils was just not used to this sort of thing.

"You'll think of something! I'll bring the group up tomorrow after dark as usual." Hans wanted to get Nils thinking more for himself, get his brain in high gear for tomorrow. He had to be ready if boarded.

Hans immediately left Tejn for his new errand in Rønne. The bigger city had many more potential prospects for lifting a couple of pistols, one for himself and another one for Nils. He realized that as the Nazis were getting more desperate, so in turn was he. Any showdown with the enemy was bound to be violent, and the only way to have a chance at saving hundreds of lives would be to prevail in such violent conflict. That meant at least being well armed.

Once in Rønne, Hans casually strolled on "Storetorvegade" (Big Square Street), the main street leading from the square northward. Hans would stalk his prey, a German soldier, any soldier, anywhere. He soon found one. A patrol of two soldiers was walking up ahead of him in the same direction. Hans closed the distance till he was only thirty feet away. The soldiers stopped in front of a bakery, and one of them went inside to shop, while the other was engrossed in the cakes in the window.

Hans walked unnoticed past the soldier, then pulled a six inch section of narrow iron pipe out of his pocket and whirled around in a flash, pressing the end of the pipe to the soldiers exposed right neck and said:

"Nichts sagen, Nicht rühren (Say nothing, don't move)

The surprised soldier froze. Hans turned the soldier away from the window so he wouldn't be able to see the fake pistol and any action. Hans reached down with his right hand and unbuttoned the holster and removed the Luger pistol and put it in his own pocket.

The next second found Hans 20 feet up the street, dashing into an alley between the stores. There was no way the soldier could have gotten his rifle in position and fired a shot, since Hans was simply out of sight. Hans scaled a fence, crossed a small yard, scaled another fence, then ran around the back of the movie theater and came up behind a glazier's shop where he quickly hid between boxes of plate glass and lots of scattered yellow packing straw.

Both soldiers had of course given chase, but were soon lost behind the stores and could not find Hans's trail and gave up. Hans pulled off his dark blue sweater, revealing a light beige sport shirt;

when being chased, the best defense is a change of clothes. He hid the sweater behind a box for later retrieval.

One down!

One to go!

Next case.

Hans ventured back out on the street by going through an apartment building, coming out the front door like he lived there. He was half a block from Big Square. He set out after his next victim immediately, before word of his robbery could get around. He found a similar setup on a street off the opposite side of Big Square and had the same success.

It was still early, just before noon, and he didn't like to travel openly in broad daylight. There was a small church just a few blocks over on St. Morten's street. Hans knew the caretaker well; she had babysat him as a child. He would go there for a visit and hide out until dark.

After an enjoyable visit, Hans made his way on the dark street back to the other side of Big Square and found his sweater. He found his bike and proceeded out of town toward Boderne on the south shore to wait for the new arrivals from Koszalin.

The night was quiet, just a slight breeze was up. The moon was bright when out, but was covered most of the time by dense clouds. The air smelled of fresh sea and sand and filled his lungs as he turned down the path to the shore. He found five bikes hidden in the usual place behind a large sand dune with large bushes in front. He added his own bike to the collection. He checked around. He was alone, and all was quiet. He lay down for a few hours of nap time. Captain Jay would not be arriving for another 4-5 hours.

At 3 AM Hans was awake and peered across the sea for the first sign of Captain Jay. Soon he heard the faint put put of an approaching fishing boat slowing down and gave the OK signal.

A new party of five was safely set ashore, after an uneventful journey from Poland. There were three young men in their twenties and a middle aged couple.

Hans brought them safely to Tejn, arriving in the dark, a couple of hours after sunset as promised.

CHAPTER 22

Nils set out for Sweden less than fifteen minutes after the group arrived.

He was ready.

No time to waste.

If they were to meet with a boarding patrol, he wanted it to be in the early evening, while he was still fresh and alert, not during the night when he might be tired and sleepy.

The people were hidden in the usual hiding place. Pointing to the middle aged man, Nils said, "I'm going to make you the key defender. You'll be placed in the hiding place last, so that you'll be right there at the opening if the cover is removed. I'm going to give you a pistol, so listen very carefully! If the cover is removed before we arrive in Sweden, you'll immediately shoot to kill. Fire one shot at the head of the first person you see, followed by a second shot to the center of the chest. Do not hesitate even one second, because then you'll be the one that's shot. The Nazis are ready for any resistance, and will have their guns drawn and ready to shoot in an instant. The only way to beat them is to shoot first, and to do that you have to be very fast. No hesitation! Is that clear?"

"Yes, I understand."

"Are you absolutely sure you can do it?"

"Yes, I'm actually quite eager to avenge my friends already killed by the Nazis."

"You know what's at stake here," Nils instructed further, "many, many lives! Not just you and your family, but also all of us and all the people that need to follow you; they must all be allowed to come. If you don't strike like a snake in the grass when challenged, the plan will not succeed."

"Yes, yes, I understand, and I'll do it, absolutely, I'll do it. In a way, I hope an officer will show his face in the opening, so I can have the pleasure of blasting him right to hell. But, of course I would rather not see anyone before Sweden."

"Good. Remember, he who hesitates is lost!

Furthermore, for safety reasons, do not put your finger on the trigger until I tell you to do so. That way you will not fire the pistol accidentally. The time to do so will be when we are about to be boarded, and that's when I'll tell you to do it. I'll tell you to place your finger now. Then you should have no problem firing the pistol in an instant, if and when that time comes. The German Luger automatic pistol is what's called a "double action" automatic pistol, where the two actions of cocking and firing are done with only one and the same pull on the trigger."

The cover was placed over the opening and secured as usual. Nils slowly eased the boat out to sea.

Turning to his crew he continued " What better place to hide a weapon than with the people being hidden, right?"

"Yeah, the two are like one. If one is discovered they both are."

"If one is discovered, the pistol will be used, and only then."

"Tell me, why did you choose the older man to be the key defender?"

"Because, the young men might hesitate simply from lack of maturity. These are moments where 100% focus is necessary. No room for moral or religious scruples or other philosophical considerations at the last minute. The chips are down. This is a do or die situation. Instant action is called for. Instant lethal force. Instant death to the enemy. If you can't deliver that, you have no business holding a pistol. That's why!"

"I see, so it'll be safest for the more mature man have a go at it."

"Right, he claimed to be up to it; time will tell.

As for the second pistol, that's another matter. What was it Hans said: Two was always better than one!? I am not so sure," Nils concluded..

"Are you really going to hold on to it yourself?"

"If we're not boarded, there's no reason I couldn't keep it on myself. And if we're boarded, I'll need it in a flash, and it'll not do to have it hidden elsewhere on the boat, where I might not be able to get to it."

"That all sounds very logical, but what if we are searched at gunpoint when we're boarded?" The crew member asked. "They'll find your pistol and shoot you, won't they?"

"You know, that does remind me of a boarding I heard about, where the Nazis came aboard with guns drawn, aimed at everyone aboard, then searched them at gun point. The Nazis clearly had the drop on them. It would've been sheer folly to try any heroics in that situation, as the Nazis would have mowed everyone down in an instant with a hail of bullets. You know, I think you're right. I wouldn't be able to out shoot them when they already have me in their gun sights. We wouldn't have an equal start as in a Western style quick draw shoot out. They'd already be ahead of me. I'll have to think of another way to take control."

Nils continued talking to both his crew members.

"One thing I can tell you, when that refugee fires his gun at the Nazi officer, or whoever shows his face to him, all hell will break loose. You must instantly drop to the deck with your hands stretched out above your head. It'll be the only way to avoid the hail of bullets that will result."

"And what're you going to do?"

"I'll think of something. Don't worry, guys, I have an idea." Nils tried to assure them.

"What is it? Tell us!"

"No, I need time to act it out in my mind first."

The fishing boat was now going at full speed through the choppy waters off the north coast of Bornholm. Dense clouds covered the moon, and no light was seen anywhere.

"Once in a while, I'm going to bring the boat to a complete stop, so the engine can idle, and the boat drift rather than beat noisily into the waves. I need to listen for a few minutes to be able to detect any engine noise from a German patrol boat that might be in the neighborhood."

When he was out in mid ocean, half way to Sweden, Nils made one of his brief listening stops.

"I couldn't hear anything," he said quietly and put the engine in forward.

Suddenly a blinding white light bathed the entire boat on the port side.

Nils knew exactly what was about to happen.

"Place your finger now," he commanded softly, knowing the refugee would hear him, being only a few feet away.

The German patrol boat had been drifting for a while, half way between Bornholm and Sweden, right along the path a fishing boat might take. It had waited there for a while, without lights or engine running, and had remained undetected. Their tactic had been successful. They had intercepted a fishing boat, right in the path to Sweden. Very suspicious!

The patrol boat moved in close, and the usual harsh commands were yelled out. The patrol boat came along side. There was an officer already pointing his pistol at Nils, a soldier at the wheel, and another at the railing, where he proceeded to secure the patrol boat to the bow and stern of the fishing boat. It was the only safe way to board one boat from the other in the choppy sea. The three Nazis now came aboard.

"I'm glad you were already stopped, Hr. Kapitan," he said. "I should hate to chase after you in this choppy sea. We heard your engine coming, but we didn't see any lights. You are breaking the rules of navigation, are you not?"

"We're merely moving quickly from one place to another and testing the water for fish. The fish go deeper in choppy seas like this, and that makes them harder to find. They're smart. We only move a short time, and there's nobody out here, except you of course, and by the way, I didn't see any lights on your boat either."

"Is that right? But why don't I see anyone else out here trying to fish? Why are you the only ones?"

"I suppose we're more desperate to fish. We've had several weeks of bad weather, as you probably know."

Nils, like most Danes, had no problem prevailing when debating the issues with the Nazis.

The officer seemed to be satisfied with the answers, at least for the time being. He began to look around, kicked a few fishing nets with cork floats attached, stomped a few times at various places around the deck, nearly loosing his balance several times. It was very tempting for Nils to lend a helping hand in sending him overboard, but he bided his time. There would probably come a better time. Opportunity would knock, and Nils would open the door!

The two soldiers were sitting down on the railing, one on each side of the bow of the boat, to avoid falling in the violent rolling and pitching. Their rifles were still pointed at the crew, who were standing at the mid ship starboard railing.

The boats bounced high and wide, as they drifted in the very choppy ocean. Tied together, the two boats made a lot of creaking and groaning noises. Standing or walking on deck was very uncomfortable, if not impossible. All that was in Nils's favor, in that even the Nazis would not want to prolong the search more than strictly necessary.

The Nazi officer turned toward his patrol boat and motioned to the two soldiers and said "Zurück" (back).

The search was over.

Hallelujah!

Thank God for choppy seas.

It was even too much for the Nazis!

Nils slowly edged closer to the pilot house, about to enter and take the wheel again.

The back door had been purposely jammed in a half way open position with a door stop on the deck, so as to provide quick and easy access to the engine controls and the wheel.

The officer started lifting his leg to climb over the two railings back into his own boat, when a loud noise was heard.

The officer froze, then turned around and put his leg back on the deck, again pointing his pistol at Nils.

There it was again.

A loud retching noise.

One of the crew quickly doubled over clutching the railing, pretended to make retching noises.

Suddenly another retching noise was heard.

It was not coming from the crew member.

It seemed to be coming from below the deck.

The officer promptly went over to the central portion of the wide deck space in front of the pilot house. There he tapped the deck several places with his foot; no noise was heard.

He turned to Nils and announced, "I think there's someone under the deck! Are you carrying Jewish refugees, Hr. Kapitan?"

"Certainly not," Nils replied as innocently as possible.

"What's down under this deck?"

"Just spare nets and an old sail," Nils replied.

"Let's have a look, shall we?"

"Open the locker!" Nils directed the crew member still standing.

The crew member made his way from the railing over to the cover of the hiding place and removed the locking block of wood and then the board covering the opening and stepped back as far as he could, returning to the railing, looking as though he might need to use it to feed the fish himself.

The officer hobbled over, trying to keep his balance as the boats were tossed around in the wild sea.

He grabbed on to the edge of the one foot wide opening with his right hand, still holding the pistol in his left hand.

Nils slowly edged all the way over to the corner of the pilot house, his right hand slowly inching its way just inside the pilot house, where it grabbed his pistol.

He had found a hiding place that suited his plan. A small loose board just inside the pilot house had made a perfect little receptacle for the pistol. A couple of gasoline soaked rags were draped over it, just in case any dogs were to come aboard. Of course, the dogs could not handle this kind of sea, so they got to stay home. Nils realized that he was now in plan B.

The point of no return had been passed.

A violent confrontation was now imminent.

The Nazi officer leaned down and forward to look at the contents of the locker. In so doing, he had to lean on his left hand,

175

still holding the pistol, but now no longer able to keep it pointed at Nils. His right hand was busy holding on to the edge of the opening to the locker to keep him from being thrown about by the unruly sea.

There was nothing to bee seen, as he peered down, seeing the old weather beaten wood of the empty locker bottom.

"There's got to be somebody down here!" He shouted. "I know the noise came from here! You can come out now," he shouted into the locker opening.

No one stirred.

Not a sound could be heard.

They all held their breath.

This was it.

The moment of truth.

Perhaps the moment of death!

It was that time again, when death was only an inch away, just on the other side of that last board.

That board was now gone.

Would death take its place?

The two men were inches apart.

They each had an action in mind.

They both had the same intention.

To kill the enemy.

They were both well prepared.

They were both middle aged.

They were both educated.

They both knew their weapons.

They had both been waiting for this moment.

A moment of inevitable confrontation.

They both represented a way of life.

One a cruel and merciless ideology of war and killing.

The other a peaceful productive ideology.

One an atheistic, hedonistic philosophy.

The other a religious God fearing philosophy.

They were as opposite as any one could be.

They were not unlike David and Goliath.

Was that story to repeat itself on the Baltic Sea?

The Nazi likely never heard of that event thousands of years ago.

Ah! Might that be the beginning of an advantage?

The Jew would know the story quite well.

And so an advantage began to creep in.

A decided advantage in favor of the Jew.

It was knowledge of the enemy!

That first rule of engagement.

Know your enemy!

How would that help the Jew?

Knowing the overwhelming fighting power possessed by the Nazi, his military training, his war experience, his arrogance and extreme self confidence.

Knowing all that, the Jew had the advantage.

The Nazi assumed the Jew was timid, defenseless, had no military or war experience, would be deathly afraid.

Knowing all that, the Nazi thought he had the advantage, but in reality he did not know the Jew. The Jew was not what he assumed. Therein lay his disadvantage.

The Jew saw the picture clearly.

Surprise was his best weapon!

Surprise in mode of attack.

Surprise in having a weapon.

Surprise in type of weapon.

Surprise in timing.

He knew he would have only one chance.

It would be an instant.

A second.

No, a fraction of a second.

In a Western style shoot-out on Main Street, he who moved first would win.

Right here, he who moved first would loose.

The Jew had figured that out.

He had been told and instructed of that by freedom fighters who knew. It had been confirmed for him.

He knew his enemy.

His enemy didn't know him.

The battle was won before it began!

The Nazi officer was certain there was somebody down there under the deck.

He bent down all the way to the deck so he could get a look under the board he was holding on to.

He was right!

There was somebody down there.

It was not what he expected.

He was looking straight into the barrel of a pistol!

His eyes widened.

But he couldn't move.

The rolling of the boat in the heavy seas exerted an unexpected force that pinned him to the deck in spite of all his efforts to raise himself and move away from the opening. Bending down so far that he could see, eliminated his leverage to counter the force that pinned him down.

This could not be.

He was the one with the gun.

But he couldn't move!

He now experienced what all his previous victims had experienced.

He now saw the end of the world from their side.

He was now the one who was looking death in the eye.

And death was smiling at him.

Death whispered, "Gotcha!"

A shot rang out.

It was worse than thunder.

It was like a mighty explosion.

The sound seemed to rip the narrow hiding place open.

His head jerked backwards a couple of feet,

blood dripping all over.

He collapsed instantly, partly covering the opening to the locker.

The Jew had gotten his wish.

His nemesis had been blown to hell or beyond.

He himself couldn't move.

His hand trembled, almost dropping the pistol.

The shock of that extreme violence in such close quarters had a paralyzing effect on both mind and body. He nearly passed out, as the excitement leading up to the shot was now over.

With a single shot, he had saved the lives of many, everyone aboard the fishing boat, as well as hundreds of his fellow Jews.

He was an instant hero.

Nils knew a shot was coming. He hoped and prayed it would be from the refugee. He readied himself for the moment. It would be only seconds away. He gripped the pistol tightly with his finger on the trigger, raising the pistol slowly till it was at the level of his eyes, but still concealed behind the corner of the pilothouse. As he heard the shot, he instantly ducked behind the pilot house while reaching around the corner, firing his pistol rapidly at each of the two soldiers, as they also fired their weapons.

They didn't know whom to shoot at.

They didn't know their enemy.

They didn't have a plan.

They couldn't have one.

They were lost before it all started.

They were supposed to cover the crew, but they were unexpectedly lying face down on the deck, and what kind of target was that?

They turned their eyes on Nils and realized that he should have been the number one target.

First then did they start firing at Nils.

That reasoning process took only two seconds, but for them it became an eternity.

It gave Nils plenty of time to seek cover and direct his pistol at them and fire at both of them.

Their shots missed Nils and went out to sea.

Nils's shots nailed them both, putting an end to their combat.

The soldiers had been defenseless against the fast action of Nils, who had carefully thought all this out in his mind while leaving Bornholm. The key feature of his plan was that the soldiers had nowhere to hide. There was nothing to shield them from Nils's bullets, whether they were up at the bow or even down by the railing close to their own boat. No cover! But Nils had instant cover behind the pilot house. Indeed, a hail of bullets went by his ears out to sea. Nils had been safe, but also free to fire at them.

The pilot house, a five by five foot square tower little more than six feet high, in the center of the back of the fishing boat was designed to shield the fisherman from the cold wind and spray of the sea. It now had been able to shield a courageous fisherman from the spray of Nazi bullets.

Another important feature of his plan was the nature of the sea. Nils was quite at home on the waves, small or large, and this rough weather with violent lurches, rolling and pitching was child's play for him. It had been part of him for many years. For him it was all in a day's work; but for the Nazis, it was a formidable hindrance for them to work comfortably and focused.

Add to that the sudden unexpected force brought to bear when someone was off balance, such as the officer leaning down on one arm. He could readily find himself in an unexpected and impossible situation, unable to keep his balance or just simply unable to move, until that force vanished with an opposite movement of the boat. Here, the officer had been unable to move out of the way of a lethal bullet, pinned down by a hard rolling of the boat in the rough sea. Nils had counted on such disadvantage impeding the Nazis. You can call it the "home turf" advantage. But it's not enough just to have that advantage; you must also be able to make use of it.

Opportunity had knocked; Nils had opened the door for it at the right time. At a time when he had the decided advantage.

The crew released the patrol boat and set it adrift. They collected all weapons, then dumped the dead officer and soldiers overboard. After that they set about to wash the blood off the deck.

Nils leaned over the opening of the locker and said, "Don't shoot, it's just me, Nils! Everything is OK now. The Nazis are all gone. They've been fed to the fish. We're all safe now!"

"That's great!" Said a trembling voice.

"We'll be in Sweden in a little more than an hour," Nils said, "are you OK down there?"

"We're OK," the man said. "We're alive. Don't feel too good, but we'll make it. Just get us to Sweden!"

"OK, but I'll have to put the cover over you again, this time to keep out any water that might come on deck," Nils said.

"That's OK," came the voice from below.

There was no real chance of further boarding. The weather was too rough, and it would be absurd to have more than one patrol boat out there in that weather this time of night and so close to Sweden.

Nils put the engine in forward, and soon they were all flying across the waves toward Sweden.

CHAPTER 23

After that very stressful night, Nils and his friend decided to stay in Skillinge, Sweden, till the next day. They needed some well earned rest.

The Nazis had gone on extra high alert as soon as they heard that one of their patrol boats and crew were missing. An intense search had been mounted. The abandoned patrol boat was soon found drifting in the Baltic Sea with no trace of survivors. The Nazis concluded that the boat must have been hit by a large wave and the crew washed overboard. There was nothing to suggest anything else, since no one but the Nazis had been aboard the patrol boat.

The whole incident made the Nazis less eager to patrol the rough waters north of Bornholm in bad weather. Nevertheless, Nils thought it would be wise to return to Tejn on Bornholm after dark, when they would be harder to detect by the German patrol boats.

There would probably be only one such patrol boat, if any at all, out there during the night. The tactic used by the patrol Nils had encountered would actually work in his favor on his return trip, since the Nazis would be expecting a fishing boat to come north out of Bornholm and not south out of Sweden.

Nils and his friend had supper with a small group of Swedes at a local pub. The Swedes were fascinated by the night's violent confrontation and the heroic success of the Danes.

"You guys sure had an exciting night!" One of the Swedes said.

"Yeah," Nils replied, "I don't want to have any more of those!"

"They were just sitting there waiting for you, weren't they?"

"They must be crazy to sit there bouncing around in those waves all night."

"Yeah, but their plan worked. They found us as we practically ran right into them."

"Yeah, but you guys really handled it perfectly. You saved your boat, the refugees."

"And yourselves."

"And fed the Nazis to the fish! Don't forget that!"

"Nils had it all figured out," his friend piped in.

"And you're headed back tonight already?"

"Yeah, we need to get back to bring more refugees. They just keep coming over from Poland. They're very desperate to escape."

"Of course, they're doomed if they don't."

"I know. By the way, tell us how the refugees are doing here in Sweden. Have they all found homes and jobs?"

"Most of them are already spread far and wide throughout Southern Sweden, but some have found homes near here, and a few of them are working in shops here."

"That's good to know. I'd hate to see them pile up right here in Skillinge and not go further into Sweden."

"No, they're not staying here, so I think the plan is going very well."

"Great!"

"Well, good luck, you guys!"

"Thanks."

"Come, let's hurry," Nils said, "we've got to get back to the boat. The sun has set, and we don't have much daylight left to prepare for the return trip to Tejn.

Any remaining evidence of refugees or Nazis have to be removed. The two rifles and three pistols as well as the four hand grenades have to be carefully wrapped in a blanket and stored in the hiding place under the deck and secured so the package won't slide out of reach."

As darkness closed in on the Swedish coast, the fishing boat left the pier without turning on the navigation lights and headed Southeast toward Bornholm. The weather had moderated somewhat from the other night, but the wind and waves were still coming from the West. A high residual ocean swell was still rolling through the passage between Bornholm and Sweden, causing small craft to roll and pitch a fair amount, even though the wind was only moderate. It all served to give the boat an extra push in the right direction, allowing Nils to use only light engine power and still make good headway over the sea. That made it less likely that his engine would be heard by the Nazi patrol boats.

Nearly two hours later, Nils was approaching the halfway point between Sweden and Bornholm. He was nearing the area where the Nazi patrol boat had been lying in wait for him the other night. It would not do to come barging right into another one at full speed.

He slowed down to a crawl so the sound of his engine would not be audible above the howling wind and sloshing waves. They both kept a sharp lookout through their binoculars for boats without lights, just drifting and bouncing around in the choppy sea.

"Man, it's sure dark out here. I can't see anything. I can't even see if I am looking at something!?"

"Pitch black isn't it?"

"What good are these binoculars tonight?"

"Take a good look at the sea," Nils instructed. "Do you see anything at all? Look right here behind the boat, as the waves brake near the stern of the boat. Do you see the frothy water on the top? It has a certain brightness to it. Sometimes it becomes very bright, if the top edge of the wave crashes violently on itself."

"Yeah, now that you mention it. There it goes. Yeah, I see what you mean."

"That's called phosphorescence."

"What causes that?"

"It's caused by energy in the algae that inhabit the ocean. They have a small amount of phosphor just like the fireflies in the forests. They can emit a small amount of light. It's very useful in gauging the size and direction of the waves coming at you from behind."

"OK, but what does that have to do with anything?"

"Well, waves tend to break when they encounter a change in their flow, like when they pass over a coral reef or rocks, not otherwise visible above the surface of the water. Likewise, if these waves crash against a boat, there will be some phosphorescence to be seen."

"Oh, I get it. So we could actually spot a boat drifting out there by picking up some of this light on the top of the waves crashing on it. That's really neat! What's that over there? Is that the light on the waves you were talking about?"

"Yeah, that's exactly what it is! And I'll bet it's another boat. Listen, I think I hear the engine of a boat a little over to the West."

"Yeah, I think the sound of it is actually blowing right down on us."

"Hey, you know what? I just realized that the Nazis were counting on the wind magnifying the sound of our engine the other night. That means they'll try to position themselves a little east of the route taken by the fishing boats going from Bornholm to Sweden!

We'd better be careful, because we are right in that same place, just a little east of the route line. It means we are right where the waiting patrol boat should be," Nils reasoned.

"What a horrible thought," his friend answered.

"Yeah, and I see the waves crashing on something right over there," Nils continued and pointed toward the West.

Just then an engine started up close by toward the West, navigation lights lit up, and a German patrol boat sped toward a fishing boat headed for Sweden.

Nils turned and followed the patrol boat. They would not be able to hear him above the noise of their own engine. It did not take long for the patrol boat to catch up with the fishing boat. A search light was trained on the fishing boat, and it was commanded to stop.

"We were not trying to run away from you, we just didn't see or hear you," the captain said.

There was one officer and three soldiers aboard the patrol boat. In a matter of minutes, the two boats had been tied together, side by side, and the Nazis came aboard.

"Do you have any weapons or refugees on board?"

"No, nothing like that!" The captain assured.

"Good. We'll need to search your boat just the same."

The captain and crew were searched at gun point, then two of the soldiers moved through the boat, including the pilot house, not finding anything.

"We know you have been transporting refugees to Sweden."

The Nazi officer scolded. "Why don't you just tell us where they are? That will make everything a lot easier on yourselves."

"You have just searched the boat yourself. Why don't you tell us where they are?"

"Oh, Kapitan, we are not in the mood to play games!"

The Nazi officer did not like to be made a fool of.

"But you have seen for yourself, there are no refugees here."

"I know that! But then where are they?"

"Look, this is a small fishing boat. We don't have much room aboard. We're not towing another boat behind us! There are no refugees here."

The captain was a little too cocky and was using too many words debating the officer. Such additional words could be seized upon and become fuel for the fire of further interrogation.

"Yes, Kapitan, I see you are not towing another boat. I came up from behind you! Or have you forgotten that? Another boat, jah, jah, another boat. Perhaps you transferred the refugees to another boat out there a little while ago, Jah?"

"What, in this weather? That would be very risky."

"Perhaps, but not impossible. Are there any other fishermen out there now?" The officer aimed his pistol menacingly at the captain, as he asked his pointed question.

"Not that I know of," came the immediate reply.

The officer turned to the soldiers and commanded, "Take another look around. They must be here somewhere. They're all coming out of Tejn on Bornholm. That town has become a thorn in our side. But we're closing in on them, and we'll find them. Perhaps tonight! Nicht war?" (Right?)

The soldiers started to look everywhere, this time ransacking all shelves and cubbyholes, as though a refugee could be found there. They started stomping and kicking at everything. They looked like a bunch of clowns in a circus as the boat rolled and pitched in the choppy sea, unpredictably throwing them off balance every few seconds.

They booted various cork floats around; even rags and nets were kicked at; anything in sight and reach of a boot got kicked. One soldier kicked the side of the pilot house as though he thought it might move and reveal a hiding place. You could tell they were really getting desperate. They must have been ordered to come back with refugees, or else!

"Look in the fish tray locker!" The officer commanded.

The soldiers dragged out all the nearly empty fish trays.

"What kind of fishermen are you?" The officer asked critically, "You hardly have any fish at all! You really haven't been fishing at all, have you? You're just transporting refugees aren't you?"

"It's been bad weather for fishing. The fish go deep when the weather is bad. This is all we've been able to get."

"Keep looking," the officer commanded.

The soldiers now began to stomp and kick inside the locker. Here they looked like primitive tribesmen performing a ritual dance as they circled the locker in a stooped posture, stomping and kicking incessantly. The only result was that a small piece of wood was knocked off the inner corner of the locker.

"Please don't kick holes in my boat. We would not like to sink in this weather," the captain complained.

"I doubt we could do that," the officer replied. He did not say it, but he was thinking: This captain protests too much; he must be hiding something.

"Let me see that piece of wood," he said.

A soldier bent over and was immediately thrown against the side of the locker by a hard roll of the boat. He scrambled to his feet and felt the board underneath him move a little. He grabbed the little piece of wood that had secured the cover to the hiding place and gave it to the officer.

"This is not broken off from anywhere," he announced. "This is a block of wood. It can have many uses aboard a boat. Let me see where this came from."

The officer stooped over and went into the locker, remaining on his feet as best he could, and stared at the far corner from which the block of wood had been kicked.

"Look here," he shouted, "this board is loose!"

He pointed to the far left deck board that was the cover over the entry to the hiding place.

"Come here," he motioned to the soldiers, "take this board up."

The officer struggled out of the locker and together with one of the soldiers held the captain and the crew member at gunpoint, while the other two soldiers entered the locker to remove the loose board.

The captain and crew were mortified.

The hiding place was about to be discovered.

There was nothing they could do, since the Nazi guns were pointed directly at them.

This officer was smart.

He let the soldiers do the searching.

He was not going to literally stick his neck out.

He would be like a true Nazi officer.

He would stay in the background where it was safe.

Let the soldiers stick their necks out

One soldier pulled out his bayonet, and instead of fixing it to the end of his rifle as in close combat on a battle field, he used it as a short sword.

He reached into the hiding place under the deck and made a couple of swipes, not striking anything.

The refugee closest to the opening had moved as far away from the opening as he could, but was still quite ready to shoot his pistol as soon as a face appeared.

So far there was no face to shoot at!

It would not do any good to shoot at an arm.

That would just serve to reveal their presence.

No, wait for the face!

Next, the soldier lay down next to the opening, so he could better reach further into the space.

He was also very smart.

He stretched as far as he possibly could as he lunged the bayonet deeply into the space as far as he could.

"Aaaaaaaaaaah!" a yell was heard.

"We found one! We found one!" The soldier shouted with glee, as he withdrew his blood tipped bayonet and scrambled out of the locker.

"All right, come out of there or we'll tear the boards up and shoot," the officer threatened.

There never was a face to shoot at.

The refugee was wise in not shooting at just an arm.

He did not want to do anything stupid.

When circumstances change in an instant, your life will depend on instant comprehension and shifting to another plan that can work under the new conditions.

It takes a quick wit to do that, so the most mature and intelligent person needs to be closest to the opening of the hiding place to handle the pistol.

The pistol, now a liability more than an advantage, was quickly passed from refugee to refugee and left in the far inner corner and jammed in place with a crumpled up scarf, so it would not be discovered or slide around and call attention to itself.

There was no point in just being slaughtered inside a hiding place, so the refugees slowly crawled out of it and started to come out of the locker.

"No, stay inside the locker. Just sit down there. That's it, just sit down and stay in there!" The officer commanded. "How many do we have here? Lets see, one, two, three, four, and five. My, my, so many in that little place! You have a regular ferry here, don't you, my Kapitan?!"

No one said a word.

"You'll all be taken back to Poland to Gestapo Headquarters in Szczecin, where you'll be shot. Now, start getting into the patrol boat over there, one at a time."

The captain, crew, and the refugees boarded the patrol boat, followed by the officer. The soldiers boarded last and untied the two boats from each other. The fishing boat was allowed to drift away as the patrol boat prepared to leave the scene. The engine and navigation lights were turned on, and all the seven prisoners were herded down into the small cabin space a few steps below the deck, forward in the bow of the boat.

All this time, Nils and his crew had been silently standing by about 500 feet away, intently watching events through their binoculars. There would be no point in revealing themselves if the boarding turned up nothing; the patrol boat would simply leave.

Nils had a feeling that with the heightened intensity of the searches, it was only a matter of time before refugees were found on one of the boats. Nils left his engine running in order to have control of the boat in the wind and waves and to quickly come to the aid of the other boat if necessary. It was a sad moment for Nils when he saw the refugees emerge from the locker and be herded into the patrol boat. He knew the die was cast. Now he had to come to their aid. A familiar story wasn't it; to come so close to mortal danger and always eluding it.

They had again been one inch away from death.

That one inch board.

The board of death.

It had been removed.

The board that separated success from failure.

The moment of no return had passed once more.

This time with dire consequences.

When the patrol boat had freed itself from the fishing boat, Nils and his crew cocked their rifles and put them over their shoulders, within reach and ready for action. When the prisoners had been hustled into the forward cabin area on the patrol boat, Nils put the engine in gear and pushed the throttle forward. He gathered up as much speed as he could, and hidden from view by the drifting fishing boat, he approached the side of the patrol boat.

Nils's boat was now a fast moving missile, invisible in the pitch black night under cover of the other fishing boat, now adrift.

Nils was nearing the drifting boat and had to go around it to reach the patrol boat.

With incredible speed, he suddenly swerved around the bow of the drifting boat and then swerved back on course toward the patrol boat.

Only seconds remained.

He aimed right at the center of the patrol boat to hit it at a right angle for maximum impact.

Nils came out of nowhere.

He came out of the darkness.

They never knew what hit them.

They heard an incredibly loud crash.

The bow of the fishing boat cut through the starboard side of the patrol boat like a sledge hammer.

It rammed the patrol boat at full speed, cutting it in half instantly.

The fishing boat settled on top of the patrol boat's center, weighing it down in the water.

The officer and three soldiers were knocked out by the collision and were pushed down in the water with a fishing boat on top of them.

They perished on the spot.

The prisoners were not hit by the bow of the fishing boat, as they were too far forward.

Nils had waited just long enough for them to be in a safe place during the impact.

They were immediately thrown into the water, as both front and back halves of the patrol boat sank within a few seconds.

Fortunately the captain, crew, and refugees were all rescued and pulled to safety aboard Nils's boat.

As the back half of the patrol boat disappeared beneath the waves, Nils's boat floated free and was able to turn around and head back to Sweden.

Nils turned to his friend and said with obvious pride:

"That's two patrol boats in one week! And this one without even firing a shot!!"

"Yeah, keep it up!" Said the other captain. We owe you one!"

A few minutes later, they sighted the drifting fishing boat and were able to come alongside. The captain and two crew members were able to board it and reclaim it as theirs.

"Are you guys going to be OK?" Nils asked.

"Yeah, we're just a little wet and shook up, but we'll get back to Bornholm and dry out."

"Good, I'll take the refuges on to Sweden. See you later."

CHAPTER 24

Hans had slept late after the stressful events of the night before. He was now busy coordinating another weapons drop. They were becoming more and more difficult and risky, because the Nazis were intensifying their efforts to intercept them. The reports of the bearded traitor proved that the Nazis were closing in on them. Fortunately, Hans had intercepted those reports, before they got into the hands of the Nazis. That gave him a little more time; time for one more drop.

"You know Rachel, this next drop has to be expanded to include explosives as well as weapons. Dynamite is the only available explosive, and it's safe to handle if you know how. It'll be used to destroy Nazi vehicles and buildings. The weapons will also include hand grenades this time, one of the most deadly weapons for close combat. It'll take four packages."

"Are you sure you can pull this off?"

"I'll find a way; just let me think for a moment.

I have a feeling the Nazis will be waiting for the next weapons drop with a large number of soldiers along the West coast. They've been getting closer and closer with each drop, and the last time they nearly caught up with us. I can't risk a drop in that location again…unless… we could arrange a decoy"

"How would that work?"

"A decoy would be a fake fly-over with a drop of something useless, that would attract the attention of the Nazis and make them chase after people they wouldn't know were not there."

"Where there's a will there's a way!"

"That way we could enjoy a peaceful drop in our familiar forest clearing and fool them once more. "

"But how can we arrange a decoy? We don't have anyone on the island that would dare do a night fly-over and then have to try to land a plane somewhere on the island undetected."

"That does sound nearly impossible. It'll have to be a second RAF plane! I'll request it. I'll let the RAF figure out how to go about it."

"Yes, but if the Nazis hear or see two planes, won't they send soldiers after both?"

"Yes, it'll have to appear as if only one plane is flying over the island. I'm sure the RAF will figure it all out.

They're very clever, and they know all about what they can and cannot do."

Hans sent a secret coded message to his friend in Copenhagen who spoke Portuguese, and who would then telephone London to relay the message.

A few days later, Hans listened carefully to the BBC evening news at 6 PM and heard the news caster say the following:

"And now we have to say thank you to all the listeners who sent us good wishes from many foreign countries like USA, Greece, Turkey, Gibraltar, Egypt, and even as far away as Australia. And then of course we have special greetings this evening for some of our own listeners right here at home such as Peter, Carl, Hanne and Rita. And this concludes our program for tonight. Good night from BBC."

The radio went silent, as it usually did when that half hour program was over. Hans smiled with satisfaction.

He got his wish.

"How do you decipher the coded messages? Rachel asked.

"It's really quite simple," Hans answered.

"The newscaster mentions two special words.

They mean nothing to the rest of the world, but to me they're crucial, and only I know what they are and what they mean.

The word Gibraltar is the code name for my friend that speaks Portuguese. It would not do to mention Portugal or anything related to Portuguese, as a connection might be detected. Therefore, a place close to Portugal, such as Gibraltar is used. That's a small British colony at the southern tip of Spain, close to Portugal. The mention of that word means that my message, relayed to London in Portuguese, has been received and understood."

"Wow, that's really clever. It's so simple and yet so well disguised."

"Right! The second word is Hanne. The special greetings are of course the secret way of announcing the time and place of the weapons drops. With the same first letter H in the name as mine, Hans, Hanne is simply the code name for the standard midnight drop the next night at my favorite site near the ruins of the old castle, Hammershus."

"They answered pretty quick, but how're they going to do it?"

"I really don't know how they'll do it. But I don't really need to know. It's probably better that I don't. We don't have a code for that sort of thing, and letting me know would risk leaking such information somewhere. I trust the RAF. They'll do it right, because they understand what I need them to do."

"I can well understand that," Rachel replied. "Absolute secrecy is crucial to these operations. A slip of the tongue or lack of security in transmission of a tiny snippet of information might give the Nazis a clue about what's to go down. That would be disastrous, and lives could be lost."

CHAPTER 25

Hans knew this was the big one about to happen.

He held a secret meeting with sixteen of the freedom fighters.

"So far the weapons drops have gone without a hitch, but the Nazis are getting very close, in fact, too close for comfort. This might be the last time our small group of freedom fighters will be able to get away with it, so it has to be good. It must be highly worthwhile as well as safe."

"OK, so tell us what's going to make this drop so worthwhile that we're going to risk our lives for it?" Rachel asked.

"I'm glad you asked," Hans continued. It's to be highly worthwhile, because both automatic weapons and explosives are to be dropped, along with all necessary parts such as timers, fuses and ammunition. Those items will enable us freedom fighters to better defend ourselves against the heavy firepower of the Nazis, as well as be able to inflict heavy damage to larger Nazi occupied buildings and vehicles. This drop will provide the necessary tools to severely weaken the Nazi stranglehold on our population.

As for the safety of our freedom fighters, I've really thought quite a lot about the details of the plan. Obviously, most important from a safety standpoint is the escape route. As before, the plan is simple.

1. Get in before the drop.
2. Pick up the goods.
3. Get out as fast as possible.

Getting in is the easiest, especially since the location will be faked to a site far away from the usual area. Nevertheless it has to be assumed that some of the Nazis will try to spring a trap, attacking us as soon as we're in the process of picking up the weapons and starting to leave with them."

"OK, I see all that, but what exactly can we do?"

"Two separate tactics will handle that possibility.

The first will be a diversion. An explosion behind the advancing Nazis would only divert their attention momentarily, but if it were followed up by a barrage of gunfire, like a real counter attack, it would keep them occupied long enough for the group picking up the weapons to make their escape."

"In other words, both an explosion and an attack from the rear."

"Yes, and the second would be for the counter attacking group to scatter. They will not just split up into two groups, but scatter into four small groups of two each, fleeing in many separates directions. They will then better be able to circle around to the main escape route and scurry over the cliffs down to the water's edge as usual. Those 100 foot high cliffs have stood the test of time. They continue to be the best escape path from the drop zone. Although everyone knows the path, negotiating the steep and treacherous wall of rock is never easy. Hand and footholds are small and slippery, also invisible in the dark. We've practiced it many times in our childhood days and know the paths well. The Nazis, however, have never dared venture over the cliffs and will be at a total loss in trying to negotiate them. They'll literally be stopped by them. Furthermore, slowly descending Nazis, groping around in the dark for hand and footholds, will be perfect targets for us and will never make it down alive!"

"So that's our backup plan?" Rachel asked, somewhat skeptical.

"That's it." Hans answered, "What do you think? You sound like you have some reservations."

"It sounds good to me, except for the counter attack guys closing in behind the Nazis. Are you sure they'll be able to get back out?"

"I was afraid you'd ask that"

"Well, you can't just let them get caught and killed!"

"Absolutely not! Here's what they'll do." Hans had not left a single stone unturned in his planning.

Hans leaned his head forward and closer to the group, who in turn moved their heads closer to Hans as he whispered, "You know we have to keep some things under wraps. Anyone of us could be overheard or perhaps captured and forced to reveal some clues to the operation. We all depend on absolute secrecy. We've all got our precise assignments according to schedule, and each one of us knows exactly what he or she is to do in various possible circumstances. So let's now split up and leave by separate paths and at separate times, all going in different directions. We'll meet again as planned, and good luck!"

CHAPTER 26

Just before midnight, eighteen freedom fighters approached the drop site from all directions. They wore dark gray and black clothing with ski masks to better blend in with the surroundings. They left the roads and forest paths and made their way through the low brush and rocky terrain.

The Nazis were on high alert. The past few nights had seen many extra patrols throughout the northwest corner of Bornholm, both on and off the roads. Beams of bright searchlights flashed among the trees.

After several days of fruitless search, the Nazis seemed a little discouraged, and there wasn't much activity on the night of the drop, good news for Hans and his group.

It was one minute to midnight, the usual time for the drop.

The group was in place, well hidden behind trees and shrubs at the edge of the little clearing a quarter of a mile south of the ruins of the medieval Hammershus castle. As planned, there was no moon, and the night was pitch black. Except for the very faint crashing waves on the bottom of the nearby cliffs, not a sound was heard.

Several minutes of eerie silence went by.

Suddenly Hans whispered: "I hear it!"

The faint growling of a plane could be heard coming from the West, slowly coming closer.

"Don't anybody move!" Hans whispered again.

Soon the plane was heard directly overhead.

The steady growling became louder for a brief second, only to drop in pitch and fade away. The plane had passed and was slowly making its way eastward across the narrow top of the island. Lots of searchlights followed the plane from a large contingent of Nazis stationed just north of the forest.

"Hey, look at that parachute!" Rachel whispered.

"Look, there's a large box attached!"

A light blue parachute had neatly unfolded itself and seemed to light up the sky as it slowly descended toward earth with several beams of light focused on it and its large cargo box a few feet beneath. Several shots were heard.

"They must really be getting desperate," Hans whispered.

"Maybe they think a British Agent is being dropped."

"Not with a blue chute, you fool!"

"Well, I guess that would take a green one,"

"Quite!"

"OK guys, keep quiet and just listen!"

Suddenly a lot of motor vehicles scrambled away from the northwest corner of the island and burned rubber down the north coast, trying to follow the plane and hoping to intercept the parachute. The roar of the motor vehicles faded, then complete silence. Nothing was heard; no cars, no people, no birds, not even the plane that just passed overhead.

Hans had his eyes peeled very intently on the western sky.

A few moments went by.

"There it is!"

A single quick burst of three short white flashes of light was seen low on the western sky.

Then total darkness.

Only one more signal would be given, if the first were not answered.

Hans immediately flashed the usual green SOS signal.

Still no plane was heard.

But there was no doubt that the signal had come from the next RAF plane. After a few seconds, Hans whispered, "OK guys, give the signal."

Six designated group members flashed the green SOS signal, directed toward the western sky. It revealed the exact location of the drop site and that the drop was "good to go".

A few seconds later, a vague swirling noise like a wind gust was heard directly above, followed by a series of four "thuds" as the packages hit the ground inside the clearing. Again the night was black and silent.

That was the clue for a few members to quickly move out into the clearing and search for the goods. Not a word was spoken or whispered. Even though the whole entourage of Nazis had scrambled down the north coast, there was bound to be a few left behind.

When a package was found, a signal of three quick green flashes was given, directed toward the West, not visible to any of the Nazis gathered to the East. This way all packages could be retrieved and accounted for. They did not want to leave any behind for the Nazis to find, but better that than have a "shoot out". So, if a majority of packages had been retrieved, any remaining ones were not deemed worth fighting for. The safety of the group was a paramount consideration. It was crucial that they all lived to work or fight another day!

This time all of the four dropped packages were recovered.

Three minutes after the first plane passed over the western coast of Bornholm, a second plane followed the same path. The first plane was a decoy. It lured the Nazis away from the actual drop site. They had now left the original area practically devoid of Nazis. Mission accomplished!

The second plane was silent!

It was a glider!

It made a silent drop.

No one saw the glider.

No one heard the glider.

It dropped four packages right in the center of the clearing and vanished as silently as it had come.

Finding the packages quickly, the group slung them over their shoulders and turned toward the cliffs.

Suddenly a shot rang out.

Then a second, and a third.

Bullets whizzed by the group, but no one was hit,

Then, as if an answer to those shots, more shots were heard coming from the North.

They were different.

"What's happening now? Rachel asked.

"Those shots are coming from behind the enemy lines from the eight freedom fighters stationed further back in the forest. They're slowly closing in behind the remaining small group of six Nazis."

"But why are those Nazis still coming this way?" Rachel asked alarmingly.

"They're not fighting, they're fleeing!" Hans answered.

"The few Nazis that have stayed around this area are way outnumbered and know they won't stand a chance in a shootout, so they are running away. With some of our guns trained on their backs, their only possible way to escape is to come this way.

But they've got a serious problem.

They're being pursued themselves.

They're clearly outnumbered by three to one.

They know they're in trouble!

They're still trying to pursue, not realizing it's the worst possible thing they can do.

Unfortunately for them, they're running right into us. We've got the dropped weapons and explosives on our backs. Those packages are full of metal weapons that act as a shield for any bullets coming our way."

Chapter 27

Again shots rang out.

The fleeing Nazis were now trapped between the two groups of freedom fighters. The Nazis began to fire desperately in two directions, forward and backward. "Get behind the rocks!" Hans shouted.

The Nazi bullets only ricocheted off the large rock formations near the edge of the cliffs that provided excellent cover for the freedom fighters.

The Nazis, however, had nowhere to go for cover.

They threw themselves on the ground, hoping that the darkness and scattered low brush would help conceal them. The eight freedom fighters attacking from the rear made their way around the edge of the clearing toward the cliffs. They were not about to enter the clearing and lose cover. Hans had always emphasized the absolute necessity for cover, so much so that it was second nature to all of them.

"Do not attack without cover!" was indelibly imprinted in their minds.

It was now possible for them to fire at the Nazis from the side, literally pinning them down on the ground.

The Nazis began to fire wildly at the rocks in desperation. They had to fight their way toward the cliffs, the only way to escape the attackers.

The freedom fighters pressed themselves to the ground as they maneuvered slowly toward the edge of the cliffs. Two of them, Poul and Svend, remained behind a large boulder and maintained a steady barrage of rifle fire, preventing the Nazis from getting any closer to the cliffs.

One freedom fighter suddenly slid over the edge of the cliffs a few feet to the side of the escape path. A deadly fall was checked by a narrow ledge, just wide enough for ten fingers to get a momentary hold.

"Help me! I'm falling!" came the soft cry for help.

"Who's that?" Rachel asked as she quickly moved toward the sound.

"Help me! I can't hold on much longer!"

"Is that you Ulla?" Rachel asked in utter disbelief, crawling on her stomach toward the edge and extending her hand down over the edge, searching for the person belonging to the voice.

"Yes it's me, Ulla. Grab my arm quick!"

Rachel groped over to the right a little and found an arm. It was the skinny arm of a woman.

"My God, Ulla, what the hell are you doing here? Never mind, I gotcha!"

Rachel locked her right hand tightly around Ulla's wrist and held on to the edge of the cliff with her other hand. Ulla was saved from slipping off the narrow ledge and plummeting 100 feet to a certain death on the watery rocks below.

"Gimme a hand here quickly," Rachel shouted, "I can't pull her up by myself."

"Here, let me take the other arm."

Hans was there in a flash.

Hans and Rachel struggled to pull Ulla up and over the ragged edge of the cliffs, as bullets whined past their ears.

"Let's get down the path," Hans commanded.

The three of them crawled quickly over to the top of the path and started down, Hans first, then Rachel and Ulla last. Hans went first so he could provide critical support if someone lost their footing.

The small and slippery hand and footholds were invisible in the black of night. The descent was done purely by feel and prior knowledge of the holding places.

Hans was half way down when he heard a gasp and felt a handful of dirt and rocks bounce off his left shoulder. He looked up, but couldn't see a thing.

Rachel was desperately searching for a foothold, as the one under her left foot crumbled and vanished, when she shifted her weight to that foot. Now she had both feet dangling in the air. She was now the one holding on with all ten fingers, her feet frantically scraping the side of the vertical cliff.

"Help me! I can't find a foothold."

Hans started back up the path to try to give her foot some support. Agonizing seconds went by as he slowly advanced up the cliff. All his concentration had been focused on the next several hand and footholds lower down, for which he was aiming. Now he suddenly had to shift his concentration back up to the hand and footholds he had just left behind.

"Hold on Rachel!" he called out.

"My fingers are numb and burn like crazy. I'm slipping. I can't hold on!" Rachel was frantic.

"Grab my ankle," Ulla shouted as she planted her foot on the narrow ledge next to Rachel's fingers.

"I can't let go!"

"Listen to me. Put your toes on the cliff and push a little bit, and at the same time try to lift yourself a little with both hands, then quickly reach over and grab my ankle with your left hand and hold on."

"OK, here goes!"

Rachel put her feet on the cliff, pulled a little and added a right backward twist to her right shoulder, to be able to extend the left hand a little higher, and miraculously clutched the ankle a few inches away. She was now able to lock her fingers tightly around Ulla's ankle for a solid hold.

"I got it! I got it!"

A good hand hold on an ankle was a million times better than a losing finger hold on a cold wet rock.

Hans had now reached Rachel's feet and provided support for her left foot.

"There should be a foothold just a little lower for your right foot."

Rachel gingerly extended her right foot, searching for that foothold.

"I can't reach it. I can't reach it, without letting go of Ulla's ankle," Rachel cried desperately.

"That's OK, I can hold you from here," Hans said. "Just let go of her ankle."

Hans braced himself for taking Rachel's full weight on his extended left arm and hand.

"I found it!" Rachel shouted with excitement.

"Now move your left hand down to the next ledge. Can you feel it?"

"Yeah, here it is."

"OK, lets keep going," Hans ordered."Stay close to the cliffs when you get down."

Hans could not be certain of how long Paul and Svend could

hold off the Nazis. If they couldn't, there might suddenly be several Nazis looking down at them and using them for target practice.

They soon reached the rocks at the bottom, and hugged the wall-like cliff as they moved southward along the water's edge.

The silence of the night was broken only by what seemed like random gunfire for the past twenty minutes. As the group descended the slippery cliffs, the crashing of the waves slowly replaced the sounds of gunfire. It was like a return to nature. The almost rhythmic crash of each wave was like a blow to suppress the evils of the mad world they had just left behind. An inner peace seemed to beckon them closer and draw them down into its watery home.

It was like a science fiction movie, where at last the survivors of many disasters finally reach a sanctuary.

"OK, we're down. Watch out for the Algae on the flat rocks. If you jump on them, you'll slide off and land in the water. Walk in the shallow water close to the cliffs. Is everybody down?" Hans asked.

"No, Paul and Svend are still keeping the Nazis pinned down."

"They're holding out too long!" Hans replied.

"How come?" Rachel asked.

"Do you know what happens when the Nazis get cornered and desperate?"

"They rush you."

"Yes, but do you know what allows them to do that?"

"No, what?"

"Hand-grenades!"

"Oh no!"

"That's why Svend and Poul are staying there too long!"

"But they're giving us more time to get down the cliffs."

"Yeah, but they won't make it if they don't leave now; it may already be too late!"

A giant boom cut through the peaceful sound of the waves, then another, then a final third, twice as loud as the first two.

There was a brief moment of silence.

It was as if even the waves themselves had stopped to listen for what might be next.

A slight rustle of running footsteps was heard, then clanging of weapons on the rocks.

The eight freedom fighters firing at the Nazis from the back and side had realized exactly what Hans had been saying just now. In fact, it was high time!

They had to take desperate measures before the Nazis woke up to the fact that they had to do the same.

They fashioned three powerful sets of dynamite sticks, each made of three regular sticks, the last one of six! They threw one after the other over on the Nazis that were pinned down and shooting wildly at the other freedom fighters. Since the latter could not be seen in the dark, and they had good cover behind the rocks, no one had been hit by the Nazi bullets.

The Nazis had lost their chance to lob their hand grenades over the cliffs and pepper the fleeing freedom fighters with thousands of shrapnel as they descended the cliffs, probably killing them all.

The dynamite had wiped them out. The explosions had also triggered the hand grenades to explode, so the Nazis got the brunt of both the dynamite and their own explosives. They were literally ripped to shreds, before they could harm the Danes. All Nazis in the area had been totally eliminated for now.

Down below, the waves resumed their hypnotic rock dance, again beckoning all refugees from the mad world up above to come on down to the sea.

The weapons drop was over.

It had been successful and highly worthwhile.

The group returned intact to the sandy hills south of the cliffs and scattered in all directions to their homes.

The Big One had been completed.

CHAPTER 28

Hans dropped Rachel and Ulla off at their home in Tejn a little after 3:00 in the morning. The girls were both too tired and wet to do anything but shower and hit the sack. Hans went home and did the same. The girls agreed to meet later and discuss all about the night's adventures. For now, they were just happy to be alive and well after a very dangerous and exhausting night.

The Nazis were more than just irate after misjudging the drop site and then failing to find anything of value at the site. The large box dropped by the blue parachute contained only a broken down lawnmower. They knew they'd been fooled.

They'd soon learn what happened to the six soldiers they left behind near the real drop site. No telling what they might do in retaliation, but now the freedom fighters were well armed and would be able to offer more than just token resistance. They could actually offer some degree of protection to their fellow Danes.

Ulla and Rachel were able to have a late breakfast together and have a serious woman to woman talk. Ulla summoned all her courage to start the conversation.

"Rachel, I really owe you an apology. I hope you can forgive me for making a fool of myself last night. I should never have been there."

"Then why were you there?" Rachel asked innocently.

"I just wanted to be part of the action and to be of some use to your cause, or should I say our cause, because it's our people's cause, it's Denmark's cause, resisting the Nazis and saving the Jews and all the rest of us. I wanted to show you I could also do something, count for something. And all I did was nearly get you all killed, and myself too! Can you ever forgive me?"

"We can forgive you, but next time just let us know in advance what you're up to. It might just save your life and maybe ours too." Rachel said calmly.

"You know, after all the events last night, I probably don't deserve any explanations, but I really need to ask you something, Rachel."

"OK, what is it?"

"You know, when I was hanging onto the ledge and a second away from slipping off and falling to my death, you saved my life. You were quick to come to my rescue, and I'll be forever grateful for your heroic action. I want you to know that."

"I'm glad you feel that way. I'm just very happy I was able to get to you in time, and glad we got help from Hans so quickly to pull you up."

"So am I, believe me! But tell me something. I know you and Hans care a lot for each other, and I kind of know you're in love with Hans, and so we're sort of competitors you might say, because I also love Hans very much, and have for a long, long time I might say, long before you came here.

So, and this is what I need to ask you: Knowing all that, and I am sure you do, why didn't you just let me slip off that ledge? Why did you even grab a hold of me? Why didn't you let go of me? Why didn't you just let me go and eliminate once and for all the only competition you had, the one person that might stand in your way of getting Hans for yourself?

It would have been so easy. No one would've ever blamed you for anything."

"You know, I never even thought of things that way," Rachel replied. "My grabbing your arm did not come from any thought process which was then put into action, it was purely a reflex action. Now, I'm not going to go so far as to say that I would've saved a Nazi in that fashion, but anyone else, yeah! I'd simply not hesitate, even for a second. If you want to think about it, I suppose I want to be thought about and remembered for something good that I did, for the good I was able to do, rather than for what I failed to do, or could've done, if I had acted quicker. And if I'm to be loved by someone, it must be for the good I have done and always want to do, not because my competition fell off a cliff! You know what I mean? To ask for Hans' love, I must deserve it, no questions asked. Be forever assured about that.

And Ulla, I'd save your life again in a heartbeat, without a moment's thought or hesitation, even if you were to walk away with Hans! Even if you were to cast me aside as a friend, I'd still save your life. Do I make myself clear?"

"Yes, perfectly clear."

"And another thing! You said that no one could blame me if I'd let you slip away out there. That's not really true. I could never live with that. My own conscience would forever blame me. It would never allow me to forgive myself. I doubt I could even live with having tried and failed. Thank God I was able to save you, not just for your sake and your family's sake, but also for my own sake. And whatever happens between all of us, I'll be forever happy that I was able to be quick enough to do what I did. I'm very happy to have had the rare privilege of saving someone's life."

"You really are a remarkable woman. And you know, you got an instant reward. Your life was also saved, not by another freedom fighter, but by none other than me, your own competitor, when I was quick enough to lend you not a hand but an ankle. I saved you from the same fate that could have befallen me."

"I know, but I really don't think of it as a reward for anything I've done. I do thank you Ulla with all my heart for acting the same way I did without hesitation, so we were both able to walk away alive. I know we shall remain friends for life!"

"Absolutely!" Ulla responded.

Both women were confident that they'd remained number one in Hans' eyes. Fate handed them each an unexpected challenge, and they each lived up to it.

The ball now seemed to be in Hans' court. He was now more than ever the one in control of his decision regarding his two women. He woke up late to the sound of the wind howling through the narrow streets of Tejn. A new weather front was passing through. He immediately began to recall the events of the night and soon made his way to the harbor to share his thoughts with Nils. He found him restoring the paint and varnish in places where past scuffles with both fish and Nazis had left their marks on his boat.

"What's the matter, don't you want to keep the memories alive?" Hans kidded as he came aboard.

"No thanks, you have no idea what those things nearly did to me!" Nils retorted.

"How's that?"

"You know I'm a man of peace. And for me to have been a party to those awful things nearly drove me crazy. And then actually ramming that Nazi patrol boat on purpose with all those refugees aboard almost put me over the edge. I never thought of doing such a thing. My heart was in my throat; and sometimes it feels like it's still there!"

"Yeah, but you did it. You knew it was the right thing to do, and you mustered up the courage to do it. You were absolutely great!"

"Thanks, but all that's easy for you to say."

"Of course, but it's true. And you know what, Nils? You'll go down in history! So just try to relax."

"I'm trying, I'm trying."

"Here's what you do. Go out to sea. It's beautiful and peaceful out there, when you're not fishing or trying to dodge Nazi patrols. So don't even try to fish. Just go out on a brief cruise. Don't do any work; just enjoy the peaceful lapping of the waves on your boat and the cool breeze on your face. Hey, I'd go with you for all that, but you should really just go alone; take it all in. You'll come back a changed man, calm and rested and ready to take on the world again."

"How do you know? Are you a psychotherapist?"

"I know because I used to do what you're doing now. I love the sea too, remember?"

"Yeah, and I know you're right. But you must've been a bit shook up yourself with that last caper, the one you call the "Big One", and the firefight. Don't tell me you've already forgotten about that?"

"No, no, it's permanently etched in my memory.

That was a close one, you know. It could have been worse, of course, but we all made it down the cliffs to live and tell about it. And those women, they're something else. I thought I had an easy choice before me, but now, in the course of merely a few minutes it's become more complex. But would the outcome really change? Rachel showed her true colors as a woman of substance, casting aside all personal feelings in order to follow a higher calling – that of saving a human life regardless of any other prevailing circumstances.

She truly is one remarkable woman."

"You used to say that about Ulla," Nils interrupted.

"I know, and listen to this, Ulla was actually forced to duplicate Rachel's heroic and selfless actions, and in so doing remained in the running for my consideration."

"But what would've happened if the incidents had been reversed: Ulla saving Rachel before Rachel saving Ulla? Would Ulla still have been as quick to do what she did?"

"I have to believe that she would."

"Perhaps it was fortunate that there was no time for thinking," Nils postulated," which could have high-lighted the two women's competition in their minds. Then who knows what the outcome might have been?"

"Yeah, but that's speculation, and decisions need to be made based on facts and reality. The fact remains that both women lived up to a frightening challenge and saved each other's lives. I know I can be equally proud of both of them. At the end of the day, those events really are not going to have any effect on my decision, except to strengthen my conviction that either woman would serve me well as a mate.

My final choice will have to be based on what I already know and have experienced in each relationship. As is often true, the solution to a problem or dilemma often lies right in front of you; you have but to recognize it. Many times your recognition of such doesn't come from applying all the logic in the world, or your efforts at thinking during your waking hours. Your recognition appears as if out of nowhere from your subconscious mind."

"Yeah, absolutely! Often you see it when you wake up in the morning, right? And then you ask yourself, why didn't I see that before?"

"Exactly, and the answer to that is, that although it takes facts and reality to form a basis for most decisions, the conclusions are often not recognized by your mind until your emotions have accepted them. Most of the time, your subconscious mind will know what's best for you. I guess I'm about to find that out, now that the past day's events have rattled some cobwebs out of my brain.

So much happened last night, it's unbelievable! I'm still trying to sort it all out. But I've gotten used to these waves of mass activity. It just takes a little time to understand it all. But I've gotten used to the wild and woolly world out there."

"How can you possibly get used to that?"

"I can't tell you. I don't know the secret. It just happens that way. I guess it's the way I'm made. Even since I was little, I always took things in stride."

"Even the two girls that are circling around you, each waiting for the other to…to…to collapse or something?"

"Well, there you hit on something else. I've never been there before."

"Me neither. I can't help you there."

"Too bad; I could use some help!"

"Why don't you just let time take care of it?"

"Time?"

"Yeah, you know, Father Time cures everything. Sooner or later, one of them will rise above the other. You just need to watch and wait."

"You may be right about that, but you see, one has already done that."

"Well, then what's your problem?"

"I think I love both of them."

"Aw, come on! Don't gimme that!"

"I really love them both; I just love one more than the other."

"Well, then…?" Nils was getting exasperated.

"I just don't want to hurt the other."

"I can see that; but you can't live with two wives, not in Tejn anyway!" Nils joked.

"I know, I know. I just have to get the courage to tell one of them the bad news."

"Yeah, please do that.

And now, I'm going to try to make my mind go absolutely blank and prepare for my solo cruise around the island at sunrise tomorrow."

"Fantastic! See you next week then," Hans shouted as he turned and left the dock.

Hans reflected on the conversation with Nils and all the people and events of the past few months, the incredible Dr. Levi, the fearless Captain Jay and his Polish comrades, the refugees, the ferry hijacking, the weapons drops, the execution of a traitor, the boardings at sea and Nils' heroic adventures at sea.

Life sure comes at you fast these days.

I'm lucky to be alive. Lucky to be able to live another day and enjoy all this planet has to offer.

What I want most is to settle down to a peaceful life with the woman I love and raise a family.

I'd better make it happen now.

Otherwise, before I know it, life will pass me by.

Yes, I have to act now.

No more procrastination.

Go to it!

That little voice inside me whispers,

"Take what makes you happy while you can. Take the girl that's full of life. Take the fiery one, the little firecracker! Live your life while you can. Live your life to the fullest. Leave sitting around and do nothing to when you get old. Go for her now, and don't ever look back!"

That's it!

I've made up my mind.

My first stop is to see Rachel.

Ulla will be next.

I hope we can all be friends.

It must be hard to take for someone like Ulla to be in love with a guy for many years, and then to have a complete stranger suddenly arrive out of nowhere and almost instantly capture the heart of your beloved and literally snatch him away from you.

Ulla had tried desperately to beat off the competition, but in spite of all her efforts, she didn't stand a chance. It turned out that both women were wonderful people. But the race was won not on old fashioned grounds of beauty and character and all other feminine qualities. It was won simply on temperament. A mutually compatible and stimulating temperament!

By just being her natural and fiery self, Rachel had won the race simply by just showing up!

NOTES FROM THE AUTHOR

Even on foggy nights, the Nazi patrols became more intense on the Baltic Sea southwest of Bornholm. That was not just because of more intense persecution of the Jews, but also because of the very secret production of the new V2 rocket a little southwest of Bornholm on the small German island of Pennemünde.

British recognizance pictures had revealed large cylindrical objects on the ground in a factory near the coast. They looked like they could be rockets. British Intelligence concluded that the infamous V2 rocket, many years in the making by the German Scientist Werner Von Braun, was nearing completion and readied for deployment against England. Hitler had promised for a long time that he would bomb London. Now he appeared to have a tool with which to do so without the use of planes, many of which might well be shot down. It's no wonder there was stepped up security in the western Baltic.

In August of 1944, the RAF sent hundreds of bombers across Danish airspace and the Baltic Sea in an effort to destroy once and for all the V2 rocket and the factories that built it. The laboratories, barracks, fuel depots, vehicles and everything else associated with the V2 were tagets.

The bombers did a lot of damage, but they managed to completely miss the V2 itself! They were moved to a new site further inland, and may have just escaped destruction by only minutes. It was from that new site that the mobile rocket launchers were developed. That allowed the transport of camouflaged rockets on flatbed trucks many miles to a launch site on the North Sea coast, directly across from England.

Several months later, hundreds of V2 rockets rained death and destruction on London. That could be called the first Terrorist Attack of the 20th century, since the rockets were not aimed at military targets, but were sprayed all over the civilian population of London. There was no regard whatsoever for human life.

The Nazis were clearly losing the war, as they were being driven back on both western and eastern fronts. They thought they had one last surprise weapon that could save them, or perhaps just prolong the war, by inflicting heavy casualties on the Allies. Instead, Hitler unwisely chose to inflict revenge on England by employing nearly all of the available 1000 V2 rockets in an attempt to destroy London.

London did suffer major widespread destruction, but was of course able to recover. It appeared that the V2 had been wasted on civilian attacks in London, rather than a better military objective of the advancing Allied armies. The latter continued to advance and eventually captured and destroyed all V2 rockets and everything associated with them.

* * * * * * *

In the Spring of 1945, the advancing Allied armies had liberated many Nazi concentration camps on their way through Germany and Poland, and so the Russians had liberated Auschwitz. The escape from Koszalin was halted because the persecution of the

Jews by sending them to death camps had ceased. Transport across the Baltic Sea had also become more difficult, since the escape plan had been discovered. More fishing boats had been involved in armed conflict than ever before.

The end of the war was near, and the escape plan was finished. Over 2000 Jews had been saved from the death camps. The Polish Resistance, Polish Fishermen, Danish Resistance and Danish Fishermen were the heroes who stepped forward to act when asked to help. Their efforts, risking their own lives and livelihood will never be forgotten.

To list them all here would be impossible, but each and every family involved knows only too well who these brave men are. For them to unselfishly stand up for the cause of freedom, the world owes them all an immeasurable debt of gratitude.

Soon it was the 5th of May 1945.

Germany had surrendered unconditionally before sunset on Friday the 4th, to take effect the next day. The war was finally over. Or was it?

The whole country celebrated with parades and parties in the street. On Bornholm, parades in all the towns drew huge crowds. My mother and I were up on the North Coast in Allinge-Sandvig, two beach cities, visiting friends, when we heard the news. My father was at work in the main city of Rønne.

British General Dewey was featured in those towns at a parade later in the afternoon on the 5th. He was showered with confetti. Wearing the blue band with the red and white center stripe of the freedom fighters, I was given a large bouquet of flowers to present to him as he drove by, sitting on top of the back seat in a convertible car. I thanked him for the invaluable British support for the Danish Resistance during the war.

The next day the mood changed.

How was that possible?

The big war was over, but a little war was still raging.

Right here on Bornholm!

Somehow in the great scheme of things, Bornholm had simply been forgotten. A day later, the Allies remembered that little but very strategic Danish island in the Baltic Sea. Since Bornholm was east of the arbitrary dividing line, later called the "Iron Curtain", between the Western and Eastern Zones of the now divided Germany, it technically lay in the Russian Zone, and the Russians immediately contacted the German Commander on the island. The Russians would be sending a contingent of soldiers over by ship during the next few days.

The message came back from the German Commander:

"I refuse to surrender!!"

"What? But Hitler is dead. The German High Command has agreed to an unconditional surrender! Are you not aware of that?"

"I don't care. I will not surrender to the Danish Resistance nor to the Russian Forces."

"If you don't surrender, we will send our bombers over the island and bomb the two major cities and your headquarters. We give you two days to surrender and evacuate the cities."

Nothing doing.

The insane Nazi commander refused to surrender.

On May 9th, Russian bombers set out for Bornholm, planning to flatten the main town of Rønne as well as the second largest and principal fishing town of Nexø.

Bornholm was still at war!

Imagine that!

The huge World War II in Europe had ended.

But it was still being waged on little Bornholm!

Thousands of people fled the towns for the North Coast to hide among the rocky cliffs.

The planes arrived promptly Wednesday morning, and for the next two days, during three hour long air raids each day, pounded the two cities and the German Headquarters. The German commander and most of his soldiers were killed.

Thus, World War II in Europe ended on Bornholm with those last two Russian Bombing missions.

They wiped out the last remaining German Command Post, along with destruction of over half of each of the two largest cities. After the second day of bombing, everyone was allowed to return to their homes, or what was left of them. My home was in a small apartment building in the center of the largest town of Rønne, half a block from Big Square. Fortunately it had only been riddled with hundreds of machine gun bullets from fighter planes escorting the bombers; no bombs had struck right there.

My father had stayed in town, as part of his role in the Danish Resistance, and had sought shelter in the basement of the building. He had been safe during the bombing attacks. My mother and I were already on the North Coast, taking shelter among the rocky cliffs by the shore.

Before leaving to return to our home in Rønne, I heard the sound of a fleet of bombers overhead. They were flying rather low over the island to avoid being detected from far away. They had large red circles on the dark gray underside of the wings. That identified them as Russian. They were headed westward, and within a few minutes, I heard the whining noise of falling bombs, but not on our island. The Russians were bombing what looked like a large freighter on the far horizon. Soon smoke was seen rising from the ship. Very soon afterwards, smoke was seen rising from a second ship, barely visible in front of the other. It did not take many more minutes before both smoke and ships were gone, like vanished into thin air.

Except, they had vanished into the water!

As it turned out, the Russians had without mercy bombed and sunk, in international waters, no less than two large freighters, each carrying nearly 15,000 refugees from Poland and Germany, all fleeing the advancing Soviet army, whose brutality had preceded its arrival. They were all headed for Sweden.

We learned that 30,000 civilian lives perished in that bombing raid on non-military ships, two merchant freighters. To my knowledge, that incident has never been reported, but represents one of many such outrageous atrocities committed by Stalin's Soviet Regime.

A day later, a shipload of Russian troops arrived and spread out over the island. This first contingent was a type of Special Forces, designed to wipe out any possible residual German resistance, if the insane commander had not been killed in the bombing raids. These troops were polite and mild mannered, treated everyone with due respect and became more of a curiosity than anything else.

One month later, however, these well mannered troops were replaced by a much larger contingent of very uncivilized occupational soldiers, who were not very welcome on the island. They were extremely primitive people, apparently made up of people from far out places in rural Russia and Siberia. They had no manners or respect for people or property and no knowledge of Western culture and conveniences.

They saw a large bowl of clear and clean water sitting there on the floor. It looked after all like the best drinking water in the whole world, after fighting their way through Eastern Europe for weeks on end.

They didn't know that it was a toilet bowl!

They were used to eating Caviar, a common Russian delicacy. They found great delight in smearing black shoe polish on their brown bread. It looked like their own Caviar, perhaps even a little finer. They thought it tasted the same!

Alcohol was like water to them. They could drink anyone under the table. The bad thing about it was that when they invited someone to have a drink with them, it was always Vodka, and they would be insulted if that person could not keep up with them in emptying glass after glass.

They were however very friendly toward children, and freely gave away a lot of their things; perhaps to lighten the gear carried on their backs. They gave away belts, scarves, gloves, candy, hats, and even helmets.

Needles to say, the population was not very pleased about being overrun by hundreds of such very primitive soldiers. My father had many conferences with both General Dewey and the British Foreign Office in London before it was possible for the British to convince the Russians to vacate the island, as it had not been a German territory. Nevertheless, the Russians wound up staying on the island till September that year.

At last, Bornholm was FREE!

No more Nazis!

No more Nazi atrocities!

No more killings!

No more fear of early morning Nazi door-pounding.

No more rounding up civilians and sending them to concentration camps to languish and die!

No more street fighting!

No more need for the Danish Resistance!

No more need for fishermen to transport refugees!

No more need for looking over your shoulder for possible spies or traitors!

No more need for protecting and hiding Resistance members or Jewish refugees.

No more Russian soldiers!

No more bombing raids!

What a blessing this peace was!

People could return to their daily living, if they could remember what that was five years before.

A new life had just started for every Dane.

There was one little job that had to be done before the peace could truly be declared.

All the women that had befriended the Nazis were rounded up and had their heads shaved.

They would stand as a symbol of disloyalty that had been appropriately punished.

They were not killed, maimed or deported.

They were simply branded in that fashion, so that everyone would know who they were for as long as it would take for their hair to grow back.

Those women underwent the worst punishment ever.

They were humiliated for more than a whole year.

Again, the Danes had insured that the hard times during the past five years were not easily forgotten.

It's simply not possible for Danes ever to forget the countless atrocities perpetrated by the Nazis on the civilian population of Denmark. Every home was touched by those crimes against humanity. Not one family could say they had never seen or felt the pain and grief. The little country of five million proud people was like a giant family. Almost every family knew everyone else, and thus a tragedy for one became a tragedy for many.

The Danes did not live through the horrific atrocities committed by the Soviets under Stalin, where millions were tortured and killed in the Siberian Gulags throughout the war years. But they certainly got a taste of the Stalin Regime, when they witnessed the bombing of the freighters with 30,000 civilian refugees off the West Coast of Borholm as the final act of slaughter of World War II in Europe.

I remember what I thought, when I saw it, when I was watching it with my very own eyes.

"When will this madness ever stop?"

My thought was not original.

I am sure many others must have thought so also.

In fact, many subsequent war movies recount events from both European and Pacific regions. The concluding thought common to all of them is the futility of wars and the frustration over the fact that the peoples of the "civilized" world continue to wage them.

There are numerous famous movies about WWII in Europe, from the late 1940's right up to present day productions that focus on heroic victories of battles and engagements, as well as the horrors of war. Although many of them touch on the theme of frustration with the futility of war, few leave such indelible impression on you as the following:

Home of the Brave	The Train
Command Decision	The Great Escape
A Bridge too Far	Stalag 17
Bridge at Remagen	Von Ryan's Express
Bridge over the River Kwai	Heroes of Telemark
Saving Private Ryan	

And the list goes on.

Yet, in spite of all the awareness in our "Age of Enlightenment", people keep ignoring the lessons of history. Some of the wisest words ever spoken are from a memorable quote that should never to be forgotten:

"Those that ignore the mistakes of history are doomed to repeat them!"

* * * * * *

One of the most poignant ballads of the twentieth century sung with great emotion by the Kingston Trio is the following:

Where have all the flowers gone?
Long time passing.
Where have all the flowers gone?
Long time ago.
Where have all the flowers gone?
Young girls took them everyone!
When will they ever learn?
When will they ever learn?

Where have all the young girls gone?
Long time passing.
Where have all the young girls gone?
Long time ago.
Where have all the young girls gone?
Gone to young men everywhere!
When will they ever learn?
When will they ever learn?

Where have all the young men gone?
Long time passing.
Where have all the young men gone?
Long time ago.
Where have all the young men gone?

Gone for soldiers everywhere!
When will they ever learn?
When will they ever learn?

Where have all the soldiers gone?
Long time passing.
Where have all the soldiers gone?
A long, long time ago.
Where have all the soldiers gone?
Gone to graveyards everyone!
When will they ever learn?
When will they ever learn?

Where have all the graveyards gone?
Long time passing.
Where have all the graveyards gone?
Long time ago.
Where have all the graveyards gone?
Gone to flowers everywhere!
When will they ever learn?
When will they ever learn?!

The ballad talks about a futile circle of passing. It's a treadmill going round and round, accomplishing nothing, repeating itself over and over again. You start with flowers; and after riding the futile circle, you end up with flowers again. But in the meantime, Death has paid a premature visit to thousands of soldiers, all human beings with grieving families left behind.

233

The haunting chorus of "When will they ever learn?" will always be with us until we all do learn.

The curse of mankind?!

When will we ever be truly free?

Our heroes must not have died in vain!

It's up to us and future generations to make sure of that!

We must never forget!

We must learn!

We must be free!

We must stay free!

When will **they** ever learn?

When will **we** ever learn?

When will **you** ever learn?

MORE NOTES
FROM THE AUTHOR

Complacency of Ignorance

Since the days of WWII and the Escape from Koszalin, the world has changed dramatically. There have been incredible advances and discoveries in all kinds of technologies, affecting all walks of life, and that has changed the lives of millions of people for the better. On the other hand, the population of the earth has also changed, but for the worse, as it has increased exponentially, and living conditions for millions of other people have deteriorated. The generations that grew up since WWII have endured several other wars from the Korean and Vietnam wars to the Desert Storm and Iraq wars, not to mention many smaller wars and conflicts that erupt around the globe yearly, and it all continues to confirm that those who ignore the mistakes of history are doomed to repeat them. It could be called one of the many curses of mankind.

Our world on this planet is a dynamic entity. With its constant change, it can easily veer off its desired path. We have only to look at the last two decades to see the frightening changes that have occurred and are still happening full blast. We have seen the emergence of misguided religious and political philosophies among oppressed people that now pose an enormous and still growing threat to freedom all over the planet. At the same time there has been an insidious loss of memory for all the wars and battles fought by brave men and women to preserve our freedom. Even the valiant fighting to establish this nation as a beacon of freedom and justice for all has nearly been forgotten, as greedy and corrupt forces continue to erode those freedoms. That loss of memory has been replaced by a complacency of ignorance, the ignorance of history referred to above. It must be clearly understood that in as much as all wars, big and small, are horrible events that should be forever banned, if that were possible, complacency and its cousin appeasement when confronted with a mortal enemy are completely useless and will inevitably result in the loss of freedom. Therein lies the moral justification for wars of defense. These old clichés continue to be relevant: "Survival of the fittest" and "He who hesitates is lost".

There is nothing as precious as freedom. All good things seem to spring from freedom. Some may believe that life itself may be more precious than freedom, but what is life under Tyranny? A life full of constant restraints, threats, seizures, plunders, persecution, and the list goes on. To many a life in chains is not a life!

Our freedoms are threatened by ruthless misguided and self-serving people that declared war not only on our nation, but on all the free peoples of the world! The 911 attack on New York was the culmination of their efforts to destroy us, and we are still at war with them. They have an agenda! They have insinuated themselves into practically every country on the planet! Their aim is clear. They wish to dominate the world. Doesn't that ring a bell? If I have to mention names, you the reader must still be asleep! Yes, there is proof of a connection between the tyrants of WWII and those of today; they shared the same philosophies on how to conquer the entire world. Add to that, today's oppressed people are inspired by radical religious beliefs not far removed from insanity, which plays right into the hands of their leaders. If they have their way, our civilization could be taken back 400 years or more! That is where our foes live and want us all to live, with them in charge of everything. If the religious fanatics succeed in dominating the earth, we could be brought back to the age of the crusades! You may remember also then, the same groups of people were fighting each other.

I'll tell you this from my experience living under the occupation of one such tyrant. As complex as people seem to be, there are really only two kinds; there is the good and there is the bad. It's that simple! If your father taught you the difference, that is all you need to know. What you do with that knowledge will make or break this country, even the world.

Wake up America!

Call it yet another curse of mankind that freedom will always be challenged. First we have to fight to get it; then we have to fight to defend it. Is it any wonder that it takes people of strong will and determination to be free and to preserve that freedom? That is why complacency and appeasement never succeed. All Tyrants have a far greater agenda than one that can be dismantled by mere discussion! Just think what probably would have happened if David had asked Goliath if he would please just go home so we could all be friends. Goliath would surely have laughed as he trampled all over David.

The Escape from Koszalin is a chapter of life from the middle of the past war-filled century. To this day it stands as a monument to the irrepressible quest of a people for freedom. It was truly an escape to freedom. It had a famous precedence several thousands of years ago, as Dr. Levi in the Polish ghetto was quick to realize. That same quest for freedom has been seen through millennia after millennia.

(Will they ever learn?). The Escape from Koszalin exemplified that irrepressible quest for freedom, and it sparked immediate action in three countries around the Baltic Sea in Europe. Hans, the Danish Resistance leader, welcomed the Jewish refugees with open arms; they would all fight for the same cause! Freedom was immediately and unhesitatingly fought for and achieved.

To really learn from the mistakes of history, it is not enough to just remember the mistakes, we also need to look behind the scenes and uncover the evidence of why they were made. We will find that power, greed and deception are prime factors. (When will we ever learn?) We need to learn to spot those factors and find ways to negate them. To use another cliché, "Head them off at the pass". Stop them before they destroy our freedoms!

Unfortunately, our very own nation that evolved into a great benefactor, as well as a nation of strength and a champion of freedom, has been beset by an avalanche of all the factors just mentioned! Our country will never be the same; in fact, the entire world will never be the same, unless we take another giant step for mankind and stop the avalanche, this reckless derailment of our nation. Desperate situations require desperate measures! I hope our people will wake up in time to stop this derailment of our country and thereby the world. Even today, especially today, we must wake up and fight for our freedoms!

Our freedoms are highly threatened by the reckless attitudes and actions that have set our nation on the certain path of self-destruction mentioned above. It is absolutely baffling how complacent everyone around us is; the public, the media, both political parties, and even so called institutions of higher learning (that used to be bastions of wisdom and learning). They all act like they don't care or don't have a clue as to what is happening, or more likely both. The current corrupt and incompetent approach to our severe economic crisis (caused in the first place by greed, power, fraud and deceit) is sweeping our nation inexorably down the path to a premature demise of our civilization. And the silence is deafening!

History has shown that economic demise is soon followed by social unrest, violence, escalation of conflicts, soon widespread anarchy, defiance of martial law, and eventual civil war.

Please, somebody out there, wake up! (When will you ever learn?) Our freedoms will soon be gone. Don't let "freedom" become just another word in the dictionary! Go ahead, call it my illusion. I should love to be wrong, but just remember me when my illusion becomes reality. I may not be there to tell you "I told you so!"

Wake up America!

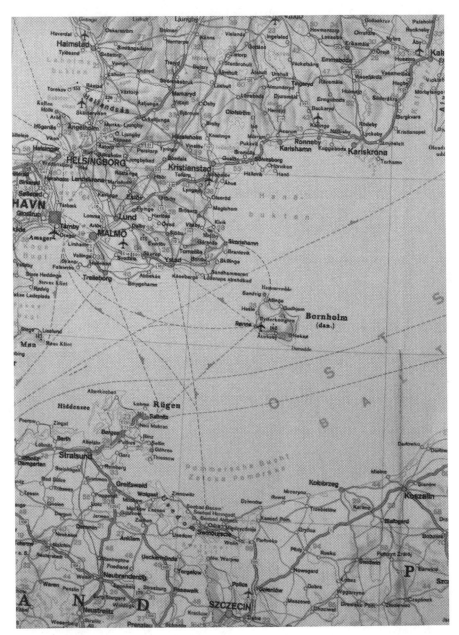

1. The first leg of the escape was across the Baltic Sea from the
Polish village of Darlowo to the Danish island of Bornholm.

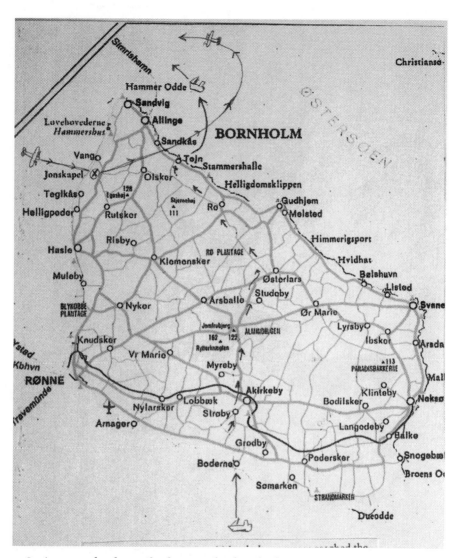

2. Across the heavily forested island, the escapees reached the Village of Tejn, then on to Sweden. The island tip allowed a safe one minute fly-over and weapons drop by the British Royal Air Force.

ABOUT THE AUTHOR

Ulf Jensen is the son of a Danish Resistance leader. He was raised in war-torn Europe and witnessed many Nazi atrocities. A surgeon in both the U.S. and Denmark, as well as an Emergency Medicine specialist, he now lives in California.